HOW TO STEAL THE LAWMAN'S HEART

BY
KATHY DOUGLASS

MILLS & BOON

First Published in Great Britain 2017
By Mills & Boon, an imprint of HarperCollins*Publishers*
1 London Bridge Street, London, SE1 9GF

© 2017 Kathleen Gregory

ISBN: 978-0-263-92276-9

23-0217

The sound of laughter followed by the slam of a car door jolted him, bringing him back to his surroundings.

He was on his front porch, making out like a horny teenager. He eased back, reluctantly ending the kiss, then leaned his forehead against hers.

"Wow," Carmen breathed, her voice soft and slightly shocked. "I didn't see that coming."

"Should I apologize?"

"Only for stopping."

"Nobody is sorrier for that than I am. But the chief of police shouldn't be caught making out in public."

She kissed him briefly before backing away. "It kind of kills the hard-nosed reputation, huh?"

"It doesn't help."

She leaned over and put on her shoes. He hadn't been aware she'd removed them. What else had escaped his attention while he let his desire get the best of him? "We need to talk."

"Not necessary." She brushed a slender finger over his wedding band. "I understand."

* * *

Sweet Briar Sweethearts:
There's something about Sweet Briar...

Kathy Douglass came by her love of reading naturally–both of her parents were readers. She would finish one book and pick up another. Then she attended law school and traded romances for legal opinions.

After the birth of her two children, her love of reading turned into a love of writing. Kathy now spends her days writing the small-town contemporary novels she enjoys reading.

This book is dedicated with love
to my own three heroes: my husband and
two sons. Thank you for loving and supporting
me while I worked toward achieving my dream.
I could not have done this without you.

This book is also dedicated to my family of origin:
my parents, who always believed in me,
and my siblings, who were my first friends.

Thanks to my critique partner, Lauren Canan,
for your constant encouragement and for lifting
me whenever I was down. You are the best.

Thanks to *New York Times* and *USA TODAY*
bestselling author Brenda Novak for giving
aspiring authors the opportunity to get their work
to editors and agents in her auction to find a cure
for diabetes. You are an example of all that
is right in the romance writer community.

Thanks to my editor, Charles Griemsman,
who worked tirelessly to make this book the
best it could be. I appreciate all that you do.

Chapter One

Carmen Shields spotted the flashing lights in her rear-view mirror and groaned. The worst day of her life was about to get even worse.

"I hope all the papers are in order," she mumbled, pulling the rental car to the side of the road. She'd been in too much of a hurry when her plane landed in Charlotte forty-five minutes late to do more than toss her hastily packed suitcase into the trunk of the car and drive out of the parking lot at the airport terminal.

Tears rolled down her cheeks. She'd wept nonstop since yesterday, when she'd read about her mother's death in the *Sweet Briar Herald*. Although she lived in New York, she had a subscription to her hometown newspaper, the lone link to her past. Her heart ached as she recounted the number of times she'd picked up the phone, only to hang up without dialing. She'd let her fear of rejection win. And now it was too late.

She wiped the tears from her cheeks, then rummaged through her purse, quickly grabbing her driver's license and proof of insurance.

Carmen glanced out the side mirror at the brown-skinned man with close-cropped black hair as he climbed out of the squad car. He looked at her license plate, then spoke into a radio attached to the shoulder of his shirt. Tall and muscular, he projected an air of confidence.

"What's taking so long?" she wondered aloud. If he didn't hurry, she wouldn't be able to sneak into the church and grab a seat in the back pew. Her stomach clenched at the thought of being spotted by her father. He'd made it clear when he'd thrown her out of the house seven years ago that he no longer considered her his daughter. She'd gotten into too much trouble and had embarrassed him one too many times. The accident had been the last straw. Although she doubted he would risk tarnishing his sterling reputation by personally kicking her out, he wouldn't hesitate to have someone else escort her from the funeral. But she wouldn't let him prevent her from saying good-bye this time.

She stifled the urge to lay on the horn, settling for peering out the mirror once more. The officer must have noticed her looking, because he raised a finger in the universal wait-a-minute sign as he grabbed a pen from his pocket and wrote something on a pad. Swallowing her frustration, she resigned herself to losing even more time. The last thing she wanted was to irritate the police. Her one and only run-in with the law when she was eighteen was more than enough to last her a lifetime.

"License, please."

His stealth startled her and she jumped, tossing a quick look at him. She quickly passed the requested ID card out the window, then concentrated on slowing her breathing. Seeming guilty was never good.

"Sunglasses," he added, taking the license into his large hand.

She blinked. "Sorry?"

"Please remove your sunglasses."

She quickly complied, folding the glasses and placing them on the dashboard.

"Do you know why I pulled you over?" the officer asked, studying her face. She looked back at him, but his rugged face, square jaw and dark eyes weren't familiar. She didn't expect him to recognize her, either. She didn't look anything like she did when she left town seven years ago.

"No." She looked away from his probing eyes to focus on his uniform, searching his broad chest for a name tag. Her heart stopped when she realized he wasn't wearing an officer's uniform. She'd been stopped by the chief of police. Of course, he wasn't old, humorless, overweight Dale Muldoon, who'd been chief seven years ago. Thank goodness. He'd been firmly in her father's pocket and wouldn't make a move without clearing it with Charles Shields first. She just hoped this chief wasn't in her father's pocket, too.

Trenton Knight looked at the young woman. "Speeding. You were doing forty in a thirty-five-mile-per-hour zone. There's a grade school two blocks from here. Plenty of children cross this road every day."

"I'm sorry. I didn't realize I was going over the limit."

"We take speeding very seriously."

"Sorry," she repeated.

Trent nodded. She sounded sincere, but a little bit distracted, as well. Something about her was definitely off. He looked at her more carefully. Young, with flawless golden-brown skin and high cheekbones, she was model beautiful. Her coffee-brown eyes were red-rimmed. Her full bottom lip trembled. He didn't smell alcohol, but that didn't mean she wasn't impaired.

He tucked her license into his breast pocket and backed away from the door. "Step out of the car please, ma'am."

Her eyes widened and she blinked. "What? Why? Can't you please just give me the ticket and let me go?"

The desperation in her voice and the sudden panic in her eyes convinced Trent he needed to take a closer look at her. "Please step out of the vehicle."

The woman sighed, opened the door and stepped out of the car. Standing ramrod straight, her small hands clutched in front of her, she stared at him as if awaiting further instructions. She was smaller than she'd appeared inside the vehicle, barely reaching his shoulder. She was dressed more conservatively than he'd expected, as well. The wind blew her shoulder-length hair into her eyes, and she pushed it behind her ear with a delicate hand.

She was wearing a black silk tank and a long black skirt that swirled around her ankles, nearly touching her shiny black sandals. He glanced inside the car. A black jacket was hanging on the hook behind the driver's door.

He put the clues together easily. She wasn't impaired. Her eyes were red from crying. Even now she was struggling to keep the tears in check. She was mourning the loss of a loved one. He knew that agony all too well. He still grieved his wife's loss and always would.

She looked at him, her brown eyes wary. "Do you need anything else from me, Chief?"

"No." Not now that he knew she was suffering.

"Then may I please go? I'm on my way to a funeral," she said, confirming his conclusion. "If I don't leave soon, it'll be too late." She turned her head slightly as if trying to hide the fact that she was crying. She slid a finger under her eye before turning back to him. "I promise to do the speed limit all the way. And I'll pay my ticket before I leave town. I swear."

Her slightly husky voice broke on the last word. Despite his hard-and-fast rule that every speeder got a ticket, he couldn't give one to her. Not today, when she was so obviously heartbroken. Even he wasn't that merciless.

"I'm not going to give you a ticket this time. Just a warning to slow down. Your family wouldn't want the next funeral to be yours."

"Thank you."

He reached into his pocket and pulled out her driver's license, glancing at the name. His heart stopped.

Carmen Shields. Carmen Shields! The woman responsible for his wife's death. She might not have been driving the night of the crash, but she'd been in the car and hadn't kept her friend from driving drunk.

He looked at her outstretched hand and then back at her face. He was surprised he hadn't recognized her. True, she looked nothing like the run-amok teenager whose face was forever emblazoned in his memory. That girl's hair had usually been a tangle of waves and curls that hung to the middle of her back, not smooth as silk and barely brushing her slight shoulders. And she'd always worn large earrings, not tiny pearls. The polite, respectful woman standing in front of him was definitely different from the rude and belligerent teen she'd been. But still, because of this woman, he'd lost his precious Anna.

"Carmen Shields. I should have recognized you."

The sympathy he'd felt a moment ago vanished, replaced by fury as the night of the accident came rushing back to him.

Anna had wanted chocolate ice cream for dessert. He'd promised to pick some up after work, but he'd gotten busy and forgotten. She'd kissed his cheek and hopped in the car for a quick trip to the store. An hour later he'd gotten the call. Now, as he stood here by the side of the road, his vision blurred and his stomach churned with guilt. If only he'd remembered that stupid ice cream, his beloved Anna would never have been on that road.

"You have me at a disadvantage, Chief. I don't know who you are. When I lived here, Dale Muldoon was the chief."

Trent fisted his hands. Dale had helped rush the inquest, something Trent would never forgive him for. That was the reason Trent had challenged him for the position of chief of police.

"Dale retired three years ago."

"Okay." She stood there, hand still outstretched, waiting for him to drop her license.

"My name is Trenton Knight."

She didn't so much as blink in recognition. The name meant nothing to her.

"Anna Knight was my wife."

Still no response. There was no change at all in Carmen Shields's expression. He might as well have been speaking Greek. Had she completely forgotten the identity of the woman killed in the accident? Did the loss of life matter so little to her that she couldn't be bothered to remember Anna's name?

"She was killed seven years ago when an SUV driven by an intoxicated teenager ran a stop sign and plowed into her car. You were a passenger in that car."

Carmen gasped, and he watched with grim satisfaction as the blood drained from her face. She staggered and placed a hand against her vehicle. "The woman in the other car died?"

"Yes. And our two daughters lost their mother."

"I—I didn't know." She shook her head as if processing the information. "I didn't know her name. No one would tell me anything."

How could she not know Anna's name or that she died? True, when Carmen had skipped town immediately following the inquest for the two teens from her vehicle who'd died in the accident, Anna was still fighting to live. But that was seven years ago. How could it be in all that time no one in the entire Shields family had felt Anna's death was worth mentioning to her?

Anger surged through him and he spoke through gritted teeth. "She clung to life for nineteen days, fighting to live. Trying to stay with her family, who loved her. But her body had been battered too badly and she wasn't strong enough to survive her injuries. She died in my arms."

Carmen reached out her hands. He stiffened and stepped back. He wouldn't be responsible for his actions if she touched him.

She paused and then folded her hands as if in prayer. "Oh, God. I'm so sorry. I'm so very sorry for everything. If I could go back and change things, I would."

"Your apology changes nothing." He had half a mind to prolong this traffic stop and make her late for the funeral he now knew was for her mother. But he didn't. Anna would never have approved of such a vengeful act. She'd been full of love and forgiveness, even for people who didn't deserve it. He wouldn't dishonor her memory by giving in to his hatred.

He dropped the license into Carmen's hand. "Don't speed while you're in my town." He strode away, determined to get away from her and the memories she awakened. But it was too late. Seeing her had ripped open the wound in his heart that had never completely healed.

Chapter Two

Carmen stood apart from the dwindling group of mourners lingering beside her mother's grave. She'd been close enough to hear the service, but far enough away to go unnoticed. Everything was over now. The preacher had prayed the last prayer and the final white rose had been placed upon the casket before it was lowered into the ground. One last neighbor hugged her sisters, patted her father on the shoulder and then left, leaving the sad trio alone.

A gentle breeze blew and a squirrel raced across the green grass. Carmen lifted her face to the clear blue sky. It was a perfectly beautiful day and it broke her heart that her mother wasn't alive to enjoy it.

Rachel Shields had loved summertime, spending countless hours puttering in her garden. While their neighbors hired landscapers to design their flower beds and gardeners to maintain them, Carmen's mother had done it all herself, despite her husband's claim that such work was beneath the dignity of the Shields name. With flowers in every color imaginable in the numerous flower beds, the Shieldses' gardens always outshone every yard in their neighborhood, if not the entire town. Rachel had claimed being surrounded by flowers made her happy. Now the only flowers around her were those dropped onto her casket. Soon they would be dead, too.

Carmen lowered her head and allowed the tears to fall. She'd lost so much precious time with her mother. Time she could never get back.

If only she could go back and change the events of that horrible night. She would have stayed away from those kids, would have gone to school and then straight home like she was supposed to. If she could have a do-over, she never would have started hanging out with that rowdy crowd in the first place.

But there was no magic eraser to remove the mistakes of her past. She could only move forward and make better decisions.

Swallowing more tears, Carmen eased closer to her family. Although she'd seen her father as he'd walked into the church between her two sisters, she was still shocked by the physical changes in him. The father she remembered had been tall and slightly overweight. Robust. He'd always been larger than life. Charles Shields had dominated every room he'd been in, throwing his weight around until he'd gotten his way. Now he looked like a strong wind could blow him over. Where he'd once been the man in charge, now he looked lost.

"Daddy," Carmen said, her voice cracking. No one turned and she realized she'd whispered the word. She cleared her throat and tried again. "Daddy."

Her father and sisters froze and then as one turned to

stare at her. Charlotte, her oldest sister, looked at her with blank eyes, black mascara streaks on her face. Charmaine, the middle sister, gasped and blinked as if she'd seen a ghost.

Her father, however, looked at her for barely a second before turning and stalking to the limousine idling several yards away.

"Daddy, please," she cried in anguish. "Please talk to me." She grabbed the nearest headstone and leaned against it, her strength suddenly gone in the face of his total rejection. He hadn't even hesitated. He'd simply looked at her—no, through her—and turned and walked away. Like she was a stranger.

Charmaine started toward Carmen, but Charlotte stopped her with a hand on her arm. Charlotte's cold eyes drilled into Carmen, enlarging the hole in her soul. "This isn't the time or the place. Daddy is grieving. He doesn't need this drama now."

"Drama? I don't want to cause a scene or upset him. I just want to talk to him." To have him wrap her in his arms the way he'd done when she'd fallen off her bike and scraped her knee so many years ago.

When she was a little girl, her daddy had been her hero. She'd worshipped him until she discovered his love was conditional. As long as she dressed the way he wanted and associated with the people he chose, his love was hers. When she'd rebelled and begun making her own choices, his love evaporated like dew in the sun. Still, a part of her always hoped he'd regret turning her away, and that once his anger cooled, he would welcome her back. But his anger and disappointment burned just as hotly now as they did seven years ago. He really had stopped loving her.

Charmaine pulled away from their older sister and came to stand before Carmen. Charmaine made no attempt to touch her, so she kept her own arms by her sides, despite how badly she needed a hug. "Carmen, please try to understand. Daddy's hurting. He and Mama were married for thirty-five years. He's still in shock over losing her so suddenly. Seeing you is another shock to him."

"And I lost my mother," Carmen added, hoping Charmaine could see how hurt and lost she felt. How alone.

"Isn't that just like you?" Charlotte snarled. "After everything you put us through, you're thinking only of yourself."

"That's not true," Carmen protested, stepping closer to Charlotte. "I know you're hurting as much as I am. I thought we could help each other through the grief."

Charlotte drew herself up to her full height, and in that moment she so resembled their father in all her self-righteous glory that Carmen could only stare. "Really? You expect to just waltz back into town and act like you didn't bring shame upon our family?"

Charlotte had always been a female version of their father, hard and unforgiving, with pride to spare. Despite that, they had been close when Carmen was a little girl. When she began getting into trouble and angering Charles, Charlotte had turned off her love as easily as she might have switched off a light.

Charles had demanded Carmen live up to his impossibly high standards of behavior. When she realized that nothing short of robotic obedience would satisfy him, she'd stopped trying. She'd started skipping school and running with a bunch of troublemakers. Although the phase hadn't lasted long, it had a devastating effect on her life. Her father had been on the verge of launching a campaign for Congress when the accident occurred, quashing his dream. Apparently, he had yet to forgive her.

Carmen realized now the hope she harbored that her sisters would welcome her back was completely irrational.

That was never going to happen. Charlotte needed Charles's approval and would never defy him. Charmaine was too afraid to go against her sister and father. More mouse than woman, she was happiest when invisible. She might love Carmen and might even be glad to see her, but she'd never act on those feelings as long as Charles forbade it.

Carmen watched as her sisters joined their father in the limousine before it sped away. Once more she was alone, separated from a family that didn't want her. Only this time, instead of being banished from her home by an angry father, she was left standing alone in a cemetery. The heartbreak, though, was no different.

Forcing her legs to stop wobbling, Carmen strode closer to her mother's grave. Her family had placed white roses on the casket before it was lowered into the ground. There were still several roses left in a tall vase beside the grave, so she removed the most beautiful one. Bringing it to her nose, she inhaled its sweet fragrance and then kissed it. She closed her eyes, prayed for strength she would need now more than ever and dropped the flower into the grave.

"Goodbye, Mama. I loved you even when you stopped loving me."

Carmen stood there a moment longer, before finally turning and trudging to her rental car. She had just sat down when her cell phone vibrated. She reached for it gratefully, relieved that she had been saved from sinking into despair, or worse, self-pity.

"Hello."

"How are you, Carmen?"

Damon's warm voice wrapped around her, providing her with the comfort her family had refused to give, and some of the tension slipped from her shoulders. He was more than her best friend. He was the supportive father figure she'd needed. She wouldn't have survived these past years without him.

She'd been homeless, desperate and alone in New York when he'd found her. He'd given her a job as a clerk in his plastics company and found her a place to live, paying six months' rent in advance for her. He'd also paid for her education. In short, he'd saved her life. Later she'd learned that he'd helped many other girls, giving them what he hadn't been able to give his own daughter.

"I'm okay," she replied automatically, and then sniffed, fighting back the tears.

There was only silence over the line, and Carmen knew he didn't believe her. He had the uncanny knack of knowing when she wasn't being honest with him or herself. In the seven years she'd known him, he'd never used that ability to take advantage of her, though.

"Well, maybe okay is stretching the truth a bit," she admitted, and gave a watery laugh.

"Did you see your father?" Damon's question, though quietly asked, blasted through the emotions she'd been trying to keep under control. Fresh tears filled her eyes.

"Yes. And he made it clear he wants nothing to do with me. He truly meant what he said when he threw me out of the house. I'm not his daughter anymore." The last words were swallowed up by sobs. She'd lost her family years ago. So why was the pain still so fresh?

She dragged her arm across her eyes, using the sleeve of her jacket to mop up her tears.

"Did he say that?"

Swallowing hard, she dug a tissue from her purse and wiped her nose. "No. He didn't say anything." She tossed the damp tissue back into her purse and grabbed another one. "And don't tell me he's hurting because he lost his wife. I lost my mother and I'm hurting, too."

"I wasn't going to say that. I'm not going to make excuses for someone I haven't met and don't think I would like."

"Good." She sniffed again. "Are you back in the States?"

"Yes. I arrived home early this morning. I only wish I could have been there with you so you wouldn't have to face this alone."

Carmen wished so, too. But when he'd offered to return home early from his business trip abroad to accompany her to Sweet Briar, she'd told him it wasn't necessary. She'd naively believed that her family would welcome home their prodigal child. Fool that she was, she'd actually thought they could comfort each other at this sad time and become a family again.

"Can you pick me up at the airport?" she asked.

"I already told you I would."

"I don't mean in a couple of days. I mean tonight. As soon as I can get a flight home."

"Tonight?"

"Yes."

Damon sighed. "What happened, baby?"

"Daddy's not like you. He doesn't care about second chances. He doesn't want to have one more day with me. Not like you do with Kimberly."

Damon's daughter, Kimberly, had died nearly twelve years ago in a swimming accident. If she had lived, she would be a few years younger than Carmen.

"Carmen, he's grieving," Damon said gently, his voice calm and soothing. It was that tone that had convinced her that she could trust him all those years ago. "And he's in shock. Give him time."

"I thought you weren't going to take his side."

"I'm not. I'm on your side as always. But didn't you tell

me you wanted your family in your life again? How do you expect to accomplish that if you don't give them a chance?"

"But what if they still don't want me?" Her voice was small as she admitted her greatest fear. She'd almost convinced herself her worry was baseless and that they would greet her warmly. Now she knew they might never forgive her.

"Then they're fools. But you'll never know if reconciliation is possible if you run away. Try to work things out. Remember, I'm only a phone call away. If you need me, I'll be on the first plane. Okay?"

She took a deep breath and blew it out slowly. "Okay. I'll stay. For now."

"Good. I'm sure you're making the right decision."

"There's more," she said, forcing out the words.

"What?"

"Remember the accident I told you about?"

"Of course I do."

She closed her eyes on the wave of pain and guilt that shot through her. "The driver of the other car died."

"Oh, Carmen. Are you sure?"

"Yes. I met her husband today." Unbidden, the image of Trenton Knight flashed in her mind. His sorrow had been a tangible part of his being. Even though he wore a wedding band, she would bet it had been put there by the poor woman who'd died in the accident. His pain was too raw and his anger too hot for Carmen to believe he'd found happiness with another woman. "She had two little girls."

Her heart ached for him and for his motherless children. She couldn't stand knowing she'd played a role in their tragedy. She should have tried harder to convince Donny to let her drive.

She exhaled a long sigh that turned into a sob. "I apologized to him, but he didn't accept it."

"So what are you going to do?"

"I plan on apologizing again so he'll know I mean it."

"That's a good start. But if you're seriously sorry, you have to find a way to make amends."

"I know." She blew out a heavy breath. "Thanks, Damon. I don't know what I'd do without you."

"You won't have to find out. I'll always be here for you."

"I know. I'll call you tomorrow."

She sat there for a while, pondering his words. Damon was right. She needed to make amends. She knew she couldn't repair the damage she'd done, but there had to be a way to be of help to the Knight family. If she wanted to maintain her hard-earned self-respect, she had to try.

And she knew just where to start. Getting out of the car, she stood and straightened her shoulders. In order to go forward, she had to go back.

It took a bit of searching, but she found Anna Knight's grave. The gravestone was clean and a pink rosebush had been planted in the center of the grave. Carmen took a deep breath and spoke softly.

"I'm Carmen Shields. I just found out you died in that accident." Carmen gulped, feeling a bit uncomfortable, but plugged on.

"I didn't know. I'm so sorry. I met your husband. He seemed sad." She could have added furious as well, but she didn't. "I know you didn't plan on leaving your little girls. I can't ever change that, but I promise I'll do my best to make sure they're all right. I'll do all I can to help them."

Having made her promise, she stood, turned and came face-to-face with Chief Knight.

Chapter Three

"What are you doing here?"

Carmen took in the chief's angry face and quickly looked away as she searched for an answer. He stood between two girls, who she guessed were his daughters. The younger one looked about eight. She had a pink sheet of construction paper in her hand and was looking at Carmen curiously, a smile on her pretty face.

The other girl was older, maybe fifteen or sixteen. She was tall and thin, with an unreadable expression, her hands shoved in the back pockets of her tight jeans. She glanced at Carmen and then sighed before turning away.

Finally, Carmen did what she'd been avoiding. She looked at Chief Knight. He'd changed out of his uniform and into a pair of dark dress pants and a white pullover. Despite her nervousness, she couldn't help but notice the way his shirt emphasized his fit torso, and then she immediately chided herself for gawking at him in front of his children. He was holding a bunch of wildflowers and a large balloon that read Happy Birthday!

A fresh wave of guilt swept through Carmen. Although she needed to begin to make amends, this clearly wasn't the time or the place. Mumbling an apology, she started to walk away. She'd taken only one step when her heel sank into wet grass and she stumbled. She reached out for something to break her fall but encountered only air.

Cursing under his breath, Chief Knight dropped the bouquet, grabbed her upper arms and helped her to a stone bench under a nearby tree.

"I'm so sorry," she whispered. Their eyes met and she wished they hadn't. Although he'd kept her from falling, his eyes reflected none of the concern of his actions. Moving to assist her had been instinctive and definitely not something he'd done out of care for her. The pure hatred in his eyes drove that point home.

He leaned in close so she alone could hear his words. Close enough for her to notice the gray flecks in his otherwise black eyes. "Don't say that to me ever again. Your regret, even if I was foolish enough to believe it was sincere, changes nothing. Understand?"

He released her arms and quickly moved away. She nodded, choking back another apology. He was right. Words didn't have the power to change the past. Nothing did.

"Who are you?" The little girl had followed them and now she was mere inches away, a curious expression on her pretty brown face. Dressed in a bright yellow sundress with matching hair ribbons on her two thick braids, she looked like an angel. Her gaze darted between Carmen and her father, who stood there fuming, clearly trying to control his anger.

"My name is Carmen. Carmen Shields."

The child edged closer. She looked over her shoulder

at her mother's grave and then back to Carmen. "Did you know my mommy?"

"No," Carmen admitted, her discomfort growing. Coming here was a mistake. She was intruding on a private family moment. She should have thought this through instead of reverting to her old impulsive behavior.

"Robyn, go wait with your sister."

"Okay, Daddy." The little girl took a step and stopped. She turned back to Carmen and smiled wistfully. "Mommy was special. Everybody loved her. She loved us a lot," the girl added, before she joined her sister by the grave.

Carmen had the feeling the child had heard these words so often over the years that they fell from her lips automatically. She was probably too young to have any memories of being loved by her mother. Carmen's regret turned to a rock of shame that settled in her stomach.

Carmen straightened her jacket, doing her best to avoid Chief Knight's eyes. "I didn't mean to intrude."

She wanted to get away from him as fast as she could. She rubbed her hands against her arms, trying to wipe away the odd tingling sensation his touch left behind.

He stepped in front of her, blocking her path to freedom. "You never answered my question. What are you doing at my wife's grave?"

Carmen shook her head without answering. How could she explain that she'd been drawn there? Or her need to apologize to someone who wouldn't hear anything she said? Did words even exist to explain the vow she'd made to the other woman? She didn't think so. Stepping around him, she hurried away.

Trent watched as Carmen weaved her way through the cemetery, carefully stepping around vases of flowers, framed pictures and other items leaning against the grave-stones.

"Why was that lady here, Daddy?" Robyn asked, slipping her small hand into his and swinging their arms back and forth.

Trent shook off his anger and smiled at his younger daughter. Robyn had inherited Anna's sunny disposition. To her, there was no such thing as a stranger, only a friend she hadn't yet met.

"I don't know."

"Who was she?"

He hoped Robyn's persistence wasn't a sign she'd picked up on his hostility and in her youthful way was trying to figure it out.

"I know who she was," Alyssa said.

His older daughter barely spoke to him these days unless he asked her a direct question. And then her answers were curt, as if she were rationing her words. Since her conversation was at such a premium, Trent was generally glad to hear whatever she had to say. This time, though, his heart was filled with dread. He didn't want to talk about the night Anna died.

"You do?" How had Alyssa recognized Carmen Shields? She'd been only seven when Anna died.

"Yes." Alyssa didn't elaborate. Instead, she flipped her hair over her shoulder. When she turned thirteen, she'd insisted she needed to have her hair relaxed so she could stop wearing ponytails like a kid.

"Who is she?" Robyn asked again, hopping from one foot to the other when it looked like Alyssa wasn't going to elaborate.

Alyssa focused her gaze on her sister, effectively excluding him from the conversation. "She's one of Mrs.

Shields's relatives. You know, the lady who always brought cookies and cakes to the youth center."

"She was nice. She always gave me an extra cookie," Robyn said. Her eyes stopped dancing and turned solemn. "She died."

"I know," Trent said, feeling unwanted sympathy for Carmen Shields and her family. Rachel Shields had been a kind woman. Days after Anna's funeral, Mrs. Shields had come to the police station and apologized for the role her daughter played in his wife's death. He'd walked away before she could finish speaking.

She hadn't held his behavior against him. He later discovered that she'd organized the women of her church to cook meals for his family. For eight weeks, a complete dinner had been delivered to his house promptly at five o'clock every evening. She'd also been the catalyst behind the ladies who'd shown up every Saturday to clean his house and do the laundry. As a single father of a one-year-old and a seven-year-old, he'd appreciated it.

How could a wonderful woman like Rachel Shields have raised such a thoughtless and reckless child as Carmen? Determined not to give the woman another thought, he turned to his girls.

"Come on. Let's put down Mom's gifts."

All discussion of Carmen was set aside as Trent and his daughters focused their attention on Anna's grave. The grass was neatly trimmed and Trent had scrubbed the headstone just days earlier. Robyn leaned the picture she'd drawn against her mother's name engraved on the granite, while Alyssa tied the string holding the balloon to a heavy rock and then set it on the gravestone. If Anna had lived, she'd be thirty-eight years old today. She'd died much too young.

Trent did everything in his power to keep Anna's memory alive for his daughters, but he wasn't sure he was succeeding. Alyssa had been young when Anna died, but she had some memories of her mother. Robyn had been only a baby and had no true memories of her own. He constantly reminded both that their mother had loved them, but lately he was starting to believe that wasn't enough.

As Anna lay dying in his arms, she'd made him promise to find a loving stepmother for their children. It was the only promise he'd ever made to her that he didn't keep. He couldn't. He had buried his heart with her. There was nothing left to give another woman.

Chapter Four

"Remember, you can call me anytime," Carmen said, then recited her cell phone number. After a moment of listening to dead air, she hung up. She'd left long, rambling messages at each of her sisters' homes. She'd tried to leave messages on their cell phones as well, but Charlotte's number now belonged to a bike messenger service. Charmaine's old number belonged to a man with a hostile girlfriend who threatened to rip off Carmen's lips if she called her boyfriend again.

Carmen sat down in a striped chair and looked around the small room, hoping something would snag her attention and divert her from the depressing thoughts that were beginning to swamp her. Although one of the smaller rooms in the bed-and-breakfast, it was comfortable. The queen sleigh bed was nestled beneath the open window. A rose-scented breeze gently blew the filmy curtains. There was a cherry desk beside the door, pink floral stationery stacked in the center.

The cozy room was perfect, and under other circumstances Carmen would have enjoyed staying there. Now it felt like the walls were closing in on her. Grabbing her suitcase, she rummaged through her clothes and pulled out a pair of white slacks and a purple knit top. She changed out of her suit, grabbed her purse and headed out.

She hadn't paid much attention to the town while driving to the church or to the cemetery. More than a little curious to see how much Sweet Briar had changed over the years, she decided a walk would do her good.

Carmen had barely gone a block before she began to see changes. When she'd left, there'd been only a handful of businesses downtown. Of those, only Mabel's Diner and Wilson's Hardware Store had been thriving. Now there was a homemade candy shop, a dress store and Fit to Be Dyed, a cleverly named hair salon. There was even a pizza place. Oh, what the kids would have given to have a pizza joint to hang out in when she was a teen.

Sweet Briar was definitely prospering in this difficult economy. It took a visionary leader with a strong backbone to bring change to a community filled with people who'd been content to live in a slowly dying town. She'd read about some of the changes Mayor Devlin had made over the past year when Damon surprised her with a subscription to her hometown newspaper, but it was amazing to see it all in person.

She strolled the streets, inhaling the smog-free air. An unexpected contentment sneaked up on her and she found herself smiling. She crossed Main Street and stopped in front of a restaurant called Heaven on Earth. Her stomach growled. She hadn't eaten anything since the tea and muffin the owner of the B and B insisted she eat when she returned from the funeral. That was hours ago and she was starving.

She stepped inside and was greeted by a hostess who showed her to a table and handed her a menu. Carmen was glancing at it when the waitress appeared.

"Hi, I'm Joni and I'll be your server."

"Hi. What's good?" Carmen asked, closing the menu.

"My brother, Brandon, is the chef and co-owner, so I have to tell you everything is good."

Carmen smiled. "Is that true or just the safe answer?"

"Actually, everything is great. What kind of foods do you prefer? I'll steer you to my favorites."

"Well, I don't eat beef, but I pretty much like anything else."

"In that case, I recommend either the poached salmon fillets with watercress mayonnaise or the salmon bulgogi with bok choy and mushrooms. That's my favorite. If you want chicken, Brandon makes a mean pan-roasted chicken with citrus sauce."

"Everything sounds delicious. I'll try the chicken. If it's as good as you say, I'll try the others before I leave town."

As Joni promised, her meal was delicious.

When the waitress returned to take away her plate, Carmen praised the meal.

"I'll be sure to give Brandon your compliment. I'll have to wait until after closing because his head is so big that if he gets one more compliment it just might pop."

Carmen grinned. Joni's friendliness was just what she needed after the icy reception she'd received from her family.

"So what brings you to our humble town?"

"My mother's funeral."

Joni instantly sobered. "I'm sorry."

Carmen swallowed. "Thanks."

Joni studied Carmen for a minute. "Was your mother Rachel Shields?"

"Yes."

"I thought so. You resemble her. I met her when we moved here a few years back. She was a wonderful woman."

"Thanks."

Joni waited a bit before she spoke again, clearly giving Carmen time to get her emotions under control, which Carmen appreciated. "How long will you be in town?"

"I'm not sure. I planned on two weeks." Carmen's stomach instantly plummeted to her feet. What would she do if her family continued to ignore her overtures? She'd go bananas with nothing to do but brood.

"If you find yourself with time on your hands, or just need to get away from family for a while, I have the perfect suggestion for how to fill it."

"I'm not a good waitress."

"Are you kidding?" She laughed. "You're much too nice to subject to my brother. He may cook like an angel, but he is the devil to work for."

Joni's words were spoken with affection and Carmen felt the slightest twinge of envy at the obvious close relationship between Joni and her brother. "What did you have in mind?"

"I was going to suggest you volunteer at the youth center. You might have passed it on the way over here. It's that huge gray building on the corner of Maple and Oak."

She'd noticed it.

When she'd lived here, recreation for teens had been limited to the one-screen movie theater or the beach. The beach generally won. More often than not they had been unsupervised. Too often, alcohol had been involved. She was living proof of the problems that led to.

Carmen was thrilled someone had built the youth center. She would like to help guide kids who might otherwise be tempted to stray as she had. But she wasn't sure it was a good idea. Many people had been hurt by the accident and might blame her for their loss. Chief Knight certainly did. She didn't know if anyone else felt that way, but she wouldn't want any misdirected negative feelings to roll onto Joni.

Carmen sighed and bit back her disappointment. "I don't know if I should."

"Why not?" Joni seemed sincerely perplexed. "I'm the director of the center and I'd appreciate any help you can give."

Carmen lifted the napkin from her lap and placed it on the table. "I'm Carmen Shields."

Joni shrugged as if the name meant nothing to her.

"I was a passenger in the SUV that crashed into Chief Knight's wife's car seven years ago."

"Oh." Joni pulled out a chair and sat down.

"I don't think he would want me to work with the kids. He'd probably consider me a bad influence, and other people might feel that way, too." She tried to sound indifferent, but even to her own ears her pain was unmistakable.

"What happened?"

Carmen closed her eyes and sighed. The memory of that night was as vivid as though it happened yesterday. She could still hear the screams, the twisting of metal. "My friends were drunk. We were speeding and ran a stop sign, hitting another car."

"You said you weren't driving."

"I wasn't. But I should have been. I was sober." But Donny wouldn't give her his keys. Still, she'd hopped into the car, stupidly believing she could make him drive slowly.

Joni pondered that for a moment. "How old were you?"

"Eighteen."

"You were young and stupid. Something all of us suffer from at one time or another."

"That's no excuse. Three people are dead." The guilt she'd felt because of Donny's and Jay's deaths was nothing compared to knowing a perfectly innocent wife and mother had died, as well.

"I agree that's tragic, but you weren't driving. I don't see how anyone could blame you."

"Chief Knight does." And her father blamed her for tarnishing the previously unblemished Shields name, ruining his plans for a political career. But not just that night. She'd begun pushing the boundaries of proper behavior long before then.

Joni reached across the table and clasped Carmen's hand. "Chief Knight lost his wife. He needs someone to blame. Although why he chose you and not the driver is beyond me."

"The driver died at the scene." Carmen knew she may not have been legally responsible, but morally she had been wrong. "I could have tried harder to take the keys from Donny. But I'd been too busy trying to fit in. I'd finally gotten the cool kids to accept me and I wasn't going to blow it by acting like someone's nagging mother."

"You can't change the past. You can learn from it and try to make a difference today. Your past will give you credibility with the kids that no one else has." Joni blinked. "Unless you'll be busy with your family. You'll only be here for a short while, so you'll probably be spending a lot of time with them."

"Not so much." Unless her father had a change of heart, she'd remain the family pariah. Perhaps if he saw her doing something good, he'd realize she had changed and welcome her back into the family. And she truly did want to help. "Maybe you're right. I'd love to work with the kids."

"So is that a yes?"

Carmen smiled. "Just tell me when and I'll be there."

"Do you have a preference of activities?"

"I'm an artist by profession. If you have art classes or projects, I could help out."

"We have an art room, so that would be great."

"Thanks."

"What kind of artist are you?"

"I paint. I've loved drawing and painting all my life. I've been fortunate to sell some of my work."

"Are you famous?" Joni grinned.

Carmen laughed. "Not hardly. At least not yet. I've been lucky." When she first started out, Damon had used his contacts to get her work noticed. But as he repeatedly pointed out, she was the one who did the painting. People only bought what they liked. Fortunately, they liked her work.

"I'm not sure I believe that. If I Google your name, will I find out you're a celebrity hiding among the little people?"

Carmen shook her head. "I paint using my first and middle names, Carmen Taylor."

"Okay, then art it is. Of course, if you'd like a change of pace, you can always play basketball."

Carmen started to protest, then relaxed when Joni laughed. "Just kidding."

"Good, because I might be the only kid in the world who almost flunked high school gym."

Her father had used his influence and she'd been allowed to join the swim team for her gym credit. She was so slow she never won any ribbons, but she had graduated, avoiding being the first Shields not to graduate high school since Emancipation.

"In that case, I'll see you tomorrow."

"Tomorrow," Carmen repeated, filled with anticipation. Tomorrow was going to be a better day.

Chapter Five

"I'm not going." Alyssa said, folding her arms over her chest. Still dressed in her pajamas, she walked around the peach-and-cream-striped chair that had been Anna's favorite and sat on the coffee table. She glared at him defiantly, daring him to correct her.

Trent bit his tongue. He'd told Alyssa numerous times to sit on the sofa or chairs, or even the floor, but not the table. But he didn't have time for yet another lecture that would do little to change her behavior. What ever happened to the sweet little girl who used to get up early just to have breakfast with him?

Deciding patience was in order, Trent inhaled deeply and slowly blew out a breath. "You can't stay home alone all day."

"Why not? I'm not a baby."

He recognized that trick: go on the offense and make him defend his actions. Not today. "I didn't say you were."

"I'm fourteen."

"I know."

"So why can't I stay home?"

He rubbed a hand over his freshly shaved chin. "Because I would prefer it if you didn't. And I don't understand why you want to stay home. You always have fun at the youth center. All of your friends will be there."

Alyssa stood and jammed her hands on her hips. "I don't have any friends, thanks to you."

She stomped from the room, but he caught her arm as she reached the stairs. "What do you mean, you don't have friends? Everybody likes you."

Alyssa's quiet and serious personality may not have made her the most popular kid, but her loyalty had earned her several true friends. She got along well with most of the other girls even if they weren't especially close.

Alyssa had inherited her mother's stunning good looks, as well as her willowy, long-legged build. Where she'd been gangly as a colt at twelve and even thirteen, she'd filled out over the past few months and now looked older than her age. To his dismay and definite discomfort, she was attracting the interest of boys who until recently hadn't known she was alive.

"Everybody used to like me. But that was before."

"Before what?"

She narrowed her eyes and shook off his hand. "Before you went and broke up that party at Olivia's aunt and uncle's house. You called everybody's parents and got them in trouble. You even arrested Olivia's cousin."

"There was underage drinking. I couldn't leave those kids there. And I definitely couldn't let them drive home. I had to call their parents." Alyssa didn't know the specifics, but she knew her mother had been killed by a drunken teenager. Surely she understood the danger of underage drinking and driving.

"As for Olivia's cousin, he was supplying alcohol to minors." He was twenty-one and, from what Trent could see, had no plan for his life besides partying. He and his buddies had given several teenage girls enough alcohol to lower their inhibitions. God alone knew what could have happened to them if Trent hadn't received an anonymous call about that party. The kids might have been angry, but there were plenty of grateful parents.

"Well, now they're all mad at me."

"Why?"

She gave him her patented you're-so-stupid look that turned his stomach. "Because you're my dad. They think I'm the one who told you about the party. Like I'm some sort of narc. They said if anybody is my friend or even talks to me, then they're out. Nobody will talk to them, either, and they won't get invited to any of the cool parties."

Anger surged through Trent and he clenched his jaw to keep from swearing. Olivia's aunt and uncle were among the wealthy residents who'd recently moved into a new development of oversize homes on a private golf course. Many of the newcomers didn't believe the laws applied to them or their brats. If Trent could have his way, the entire subdivision would be razed and the owners sent back where they came from.

"How long has this been going on?"

Tears began to roll down Alyssa's face, and it broke Trent's heart. Her chin wobbled and her voice shook. "It started last week. Brooke still talked to me, but none of the other kids did. They wouldn't even sit at the same lunch table with me. But school's out now and Brooke's spending the summer in Colorado with her father."

"It'll get better. You'll see. Now go ahead and get dressed." He tried to pull her into a hug, but she jerked away.

"You're making me go? Even after what I told you? You don't care about me or how I feel." Her words, filled with both accusation and betrayal, were a knife plunged in his heart.

"Of course I care. But you can't hide. You did nothing wrong. And your friends will come around. Just give them a chance."

"They had a chance. They're not my friends anymore. They hate me. And I hate you." The knife twisted.

Trent stood frozen as Alyssa raced up the stairs. A moment later he heard her bedroom door slam. He leaned against the banister and sucked in a breath. Although he knew Alyssa's words were spoken out of pain, they still hurt. He'd never imagined a child of his would say she hated him.

The argument echoing in his head, Trent returned to the living room. He opened the floral curtains Anna had chosen so many years ago, letting in the morning sunlight. Unfortunately, the light did nothing to brighten the gloom in his soul.

He dropped onto the sofa and closed his eyes. His sweet girl was being ostracized. Those brats should be glad he and his officers broke up the party, saving them from themselves. They might be too young to understand the danger they'd put themselves in, but they were old enough to know better than to make his daughter a scapegoat.

He heard the clatter of little feet running down the stairs and into the living room.

"I'm ready to go," Robyn announced, flying into the room. Her brilliant smile warmed his heart and made breathing easier. "How do I look?"

He smothered a grin. His baby loved fashionable clothes.

She looked adorable in white denim shorts with pink flowered appliqué on the pockets and a matching T-shirt. Even her gym shoes were pink. Alyssa had combed her hair and added flowered pink barrettes to her ponytails. Pink earrings completed her ensemble. "You look like the cover of a magazine."

Robyn grinned and gave him a big hug.

Five minutes later Alyssa returned, dressed in a short denim skirt and orange tank top. Although he wished she had chosen something different, he bit his tongue. Fighting over her clothes only increased the tension between them.

Robyn chattered happily on the short drive to the center, filling the silence between Alyssa and Trent. As he pulled into a parking spot, he received a call from the dispatcher. Trent spoke briefly into his radio before hustling the girls from the car.

A semitrailer had collided with an SUV on the highway leading into town, setting off a chain reaction involving at least seven vehicles. He didn't know what the truck was carrying, but the driver had lost his load. Worse, there were reports of injuries, some life-threatening.

"I have an emergency, so I won't be able to get you girls settled," Trent said apologetically as he signed them in. The gray-haired woman seated behind the reception desk assured him she would get his daughters into their proper groups.

"I'll pick you up at four," Trent promised. He kissed Robyn's cheek, then stepped back. He'd learned from painful experience not to show affection to Alyssa in public.

"Bye, Daddy," Robyn exclaimed, then hurried off to join a group of girls her age.

Alyssa simply stood with her eyes downcast, her arms across her chest. She heaved a sigh and turned her back to him. He wished he could say something to make her feel better, but nothing came to mind. Besides, he needed to get to the scene of the accident.

The grandmotherly woman caught his eye and nodded. "Go ahead and leave, Chief. She'll be fine. I'll make sure she gets in with a group of kids."

Having no choice, Trent took one last look at Alyssa, who was now staring out the window, and trotted out the door to his vehicle. He hoped he was right and that her friends would welcome her again.

Carmen put the finishing touches on her art project, then stepped back to get a final look at it. Not bad considering she hadn't sculpted anything in years. She hadn't known what type of material she would find, so she'd planned a variety of projects to interest kids of all ages. She'd been pleasantly surprised by the supplies at the center.

As expected, there was paint, brushes and paper. But there also was clay, string, foil, beads and other items needed to make jewelry.

She heard a knock on the open door. "You open for business?"

Carmen smiled at Joni and looked down at the little girls clustered around her. "You bet. Come on in."

"I've got four budding artists for you. Mia and Maya are twins. This is Juliet. And finally Robyn. They're really excited to do crafts with you."

Carmen managed to hide her shock at seeing the chief's daughter again so soon. Given his dislike of Carmen, she couldn't imagine he would want her near his child. She wondered how long it would be before news of her volunteering at the center reached his ears. This being Sweet Briar, she bet it would be under forty-eight hours.

"I remember you. We saw you at the cemetery. I'm Robyn."

"I remember you, too. You look so cute today." The young girl giggled and preened while Carmen quickly complimented the other girls so they wouldn't feel left out. And they did look adorable in their short sets and eager smiles. "Are you ready to have fun?"

"Yes," they answered loudly.

"Well, then, let's get started." After each girl had chosen a bright smock from the rainbow selection hanging on hooks by the door, she led them to a table where supplies were arranged. She grabbed a hunk of clay and kneaded it while explaining the project. She then stepped back as the girls charged toward the table. Well, three of the girls charged. Robyn held back.

"Is everything okay?"

Robyn shook her head. "I've never done this before. I don't know how."

"That's okay," Carmen said, giving an encouraging smile. "Just jump right in. Art is supposed to be fun."

Robyn gnawed on her bottom lip. "What if I do it wrong?"

"Oh, sweetie, it's art. There is no right or wrong."

"Everything has a right or wrong. The only people who don't believe that are the ones doing wrong."

Wow. Carmen was surprised to hear such judgmental words coming out of the mouth of one so young and innocent. She had no doubt Robyn was parroting what she heard regularly, just as she'd done at the cemetery. "That may be true in some things, but trust me, there is no way for you to get this art project wrong. Whatever you do will be beautiful."

"What if I mess it up?"

Carmen had not expected to have to counsel kids. If she'd known it would be this hard to get a kid to use clay, string and paint, she might have taken her chances with the boys currently engaged in a raucous game of basketball.

But she needed to reach this child. She'd grown up with pressure to live up to the Shields name and had cracked big-time. If she could help this girl avoid the same fate, it might be worth what she'd endured.

She knelt down so that she and Robyn were eye to eye and took the little girl's hands. "If you mess it up, we can fix it. That's the beautiful thing about art. You can work around the mistakes so that they look intentional."

"I don't know." The little girl looked longingly at the table where her friends were elbow-deep in clay. Someone had knocked over a plastic cup of yellow paint, and a saturated paper towel lay forgotten in the middle of the puddle. Apparently, Robyn's friends didn't share her fear of making mistakes. And they definitely had no interest in cleaning up their messes.

"Well, I do. Let's get you started on your flower." Carmen pinched off a bit of clay and handed it to Robyn, giving the girl an encouraging smile. She then grabbed a hunk of clay for herself and began working it. After a brief hesitation, Robyn grabbed her clay and started to pound it into shape.

"Like this?" she asked, her little hands kneading the clay.

"Just like that." Carmen offered the child a rolling pin. "Make it flat. It'll be easier for you to shape."

Robyn's brow wrinkled in concentration as she worked. A few minutes later she grinned. "It's working."

"Yes, it is."

"This is fun," she said, giggling.

"I knew you could do it."

Carmen circled the room, checking the progress of the other budding artists and helping newcomers get started. She gave a word of encouragement here and there, but for the most part, she stood back and let the kids create their masterpieces without interfering. The noise level stayed at a steady murmur punctuated by bursts of laughter. Although Carmen chatted with the other children, her attention never strayed far from Robyn.

The kids' enthusiasm was contagious and ideas began bubbling inside her. Most of the kids in her room were grammar school age. But she really wanted to attract the older crowd. And she had just the thing to do so.

Joni had given her what she'd called the ten-cent tour that morning. The center was equipped with everything from a computer lab to a gym with a full-size basketball court, and a six-lane pool. Although all the walls were clean and painted bright colors, the decor was unimaginative.

Carmen had offered to design a mural for each of the rooms and one big one for the exterior of the building. Joni had quickly accepted. Carmen would have a better chance of getting older teens involved in art if they worked on something more exciting than the Popsicle sticks and spray-painted macaroni the six-year-olds loved. Murals would definitely do the trick.

She made her way back to Robyn, who was frowning at her project. The little girl noticed Carmen and her bottom lip trembled. She swiped at her eyes. "I messed it up. It's ruined."

"It's not ruined. We can fix it. And if not, you can make another one."

"I don't know. Daddy always says to do it right the first time because life doesn't give you a do-over."

"That's true in a lot of things, but not art."

"Are you sure? Because that's not what Daddy says and my daddy is smart."

"I'm positive. I'm sure your daddy wasn't talking about art. He's not an artist, too, is he?"

Robyn shook her head. "He's a policeman."

"Right. So he probably doesn't use paint and clay at work."

Robyn giggled. "That would be silly."

"It certainly would. Policemen know about criminals breaking the law and looking for excuses to escape punishment."

Robyn nodded. "I heard him tell Officer Roberts that Peter Richards keeps making messes for his parents to clean up. Daddy said one day Peter's going to make a mess no one can fix. He said Peter's parents should stop making excuses for him. Daddy said Peter—"

Carmen raised her hand and the little girl stopped her recitation of overheard and misunderstood conversation. "I think your daddy was talking about criminals and not art. And he certainly didn't mean you."

"Really?"

"Really."

"Okay." Robyn smiled, her eyes bright with hope.

Carmen took the blob of paint and string and clay from the little girl and turned it this way and that, studying it from all angles. Try as she might, she couldn't figure out what it was supposed to be. It didn't look a thing like her sample. Of course, she couldn't admit that or Robyn would be crushed.

"I think we can totally make this work. If you're willing."

Robyn nodded.

"Then let's get busy."

Twenty minutes later, Robyn stared at her project with what could be described only as awed disbelief. "Did I really make that?"

"You did. All by yourself." If Robyn hadn't been so insecure, Carmen would have trashed the first project and started from scratch. Instead, after diagnosing the problem, she had quickly returned the clay to the child's hands.

Although Carmen added instruction and encouragement, she made sure that Robyn did all the work. Now the glow of pride on the child's face was truly earned.

"I can't wait to show it to Daddy. He's going to love it."

"He will. Now let's let it dry for a while."

The little girl started out the door. She hesitated, then ran back, giving Carmen a tight hug. The feel of the little girl's arms warmed Carmen's heart. She could start to care for this motherless child quite easily. And wouldn't that be a mess no amount of paper towels could clean up.

Chapter Six

Trent checked his watch as he stepped into the youth center. It was half past six, but he hadn't been able to get away any sooner. The accident had been one of the worst he'd seen. The elderly driver of a sedan had suffered a fatal heart attack and swerved into a lane of oncoming traffic, cutting off an 18-wheeler. The result was a ten-car pileup with dozens of injuries, some requiring hospitalization.

There was still work to be done, but he'd left it in the capable hands of his sergeant. As a single father, Trent couldn't stay at the office all night. Even if he didn't have family obligations, working the case day and night wouldn't be good. If he was too tired, he might make careless mistakes. The best thing for everyone was for him to let the second shift take over.

It was at times like this, times of great tragedy and devastation, that he missed Anna more than ever. She'd been the perfect cop's wife. She'd been supportive, listening as he unburdened himself of the horrors that far too often were part of his job. Unlike most women, she hadn't expected him to be strong and stoic day and night. Anna had known there was a flesh-and-blood man beneath the uniform. There'd been no one to fill that role since her death. After seven long years, he'd come to accept that there never would be.

As he walked through the hall, he noticed that most of the younger children were gone, although he could hear the sounds of a basketball game. Those boys would play ball day and night if given the chance.

When he'd realized he wasn't going to be finished by four, he'd called ahead, letting a volunteer know he would be arriving late, so his girls wouldn't worry. No doubt Alyssa would be even more irritated with him for having to stay at the center so long. He hoped today wasn't indicative of the summer months to come.

He had to come up with a better solution. He couldn't leave his daughters here all day and he wasn't willing to leave them home alone. Even the best of kids got into trouble when they weren't supervised. Unfortunately, his housekeeper had left two days ago to help her daughter, who was having a difficult pregnancy. He didn't expect her to come back from Tennessee before September.

Sighing, Trent reached for the clipboard to sign out his daughters and nodded at the young man standing behind the desk. He was glad to see that the female volunteer from earlier had been replaced with this guy, who nearly matched his own six-foot-three-inch height. Although Sweet Briar was a small town, it had its share of crime. Most of it was petty and nonviolent, but with the influx of newcomers and vacationers, it never hurt to be careful.

He heard the pounding of small feet moments before his younger daughter burst into the lobby, a smile on her face. She stopped in front of him, a plastic bag clutched in her hands. "Daddy. Wait until you see what I made today in art."

"What is it?"

"Close your eyes," she commanded, and he quickly complied, even though he was so tired he could sleep standing up. He heard the whisper of the bag being opened. "Okay, now you can look."

"Wow," he exclaimed, seriously impressed by the three-dimensional flower in her hand. Over the years he'd become used to finger-painted pictures and cotton ball snowmen glued to construction paper. He'd always made suitable noises about how wonderful each project had been and then taped it to the refrigerator.

But this project was really good.

"Did you make this?"

"Yep. I did it all by myself. Well, the teacher helped a little bit."

"It's excellent."

"I didn't think I could do it, but I did. At first she was telling me what to do, but when I didn't understand, she made her own project and showed me how. She said that only my hands could touch my flower. At least when I was making it. You can touch it now."

Smart woman. He wondered which of the volunteers had worked with her. He'd find out and make a point to thank her tomorrow. Now he just wanted to go home and grab some dinner.

"She's really nice, Daddy. And pretty."

He managed not to grimace. Was his daughter matchmaking again? From the time Robyn turned three and realized her friends had daddies and mommies, she'd been on a mission to find herself a mommy. Her taste had been less than discriminating. She'd tried to marry him off to her kindergarten teacher, which would have been funny except Harriet Bowman had been *his* kindergarten teacher. And she'd been pretty old then.

Two years ago Robyn had tried to set him up with her friend Juliet's mother, despite the fact that the woman was happily married. It had taken some doing, but he'd gotten Robyn to understand that mommies couldn't be shared by two daddies. Since then, she'd been on the prowl for single women to fill the role of mommy. He hoped she hadn't embarrassed the volunteer by asking her to marry him like she'd done last summer with a ticket taker at the zoo.

He'd tried explaining that he needed to find his own wife. Robyn was unimpressed with his efforts, although she hadn't used those words. She'd simply told him that since he couldn't do it on his own, she'd help. The same way he'd helped her learn how to tie her shoes. As if finding a woman who would make his heart sing was as easy as making two loops and knotting them.

"Don't you want to say hi to her?"

Not if Robyn had made the woman believe he was looking for a wife. No one could take Anna's place. It wouldn't be right to let a woman believe there was room in his heart for someone else when there wasn't. "Sure. I'll make a point to do just that the next time she's here."

Robyn grabbed his hand and tugged it. "Silly Daddy. She's here now."

"Really?" Spending the entire day here went above and beyond the call of duty. Perhaps she'd left early and come back to help with the older kids tonight.

"Yep."

He let Robyn pull him farther into the building, past Alyssa, who had her arms crossed over her chest. It was rapidly becoming her regular pose. If the scowl on her face was any indication, tonight was not going to be the restful night he'd hoped for.

"Where are you guys going? I'm ready to go home."

"I want Daddy to say hi to my art teacher."

Alyssa rolled her eyes. She'd also tried to convince Robyn to stop shopping for a mommy. Her less than subtle efforts had been as unsuccessful as his more diplomatic methods. "Do you have to do it now? It's not like this is our last day here. And besides, he's already met her." Despite her complaining, Alyssa trailed along.

"So? They didn't get to talk before. Now they can. He can even ask her for a date, since she's not married."

Trent groaned. He could only imagine what Robyn had shared about him to get that bit of information.

He allowed her to drag him by the hand until they entered a large room filled with tables. There was only one person in the room.

"Here she is."

Trent's gaze followed his daughter's outstretched hand. The woman had her back to them. And uninterested as he was, he had to admit that she had a nice figure. Petite and dressed in jeans that hugged her curvy body and a T-shirt that revealed a tiny waist, the woman was cleaning paintbrushes in the sink. Humming softly to herself, she didn't hear them approach.

"Miss Shields. Daddy came to say hi to you. Don't you think he's handsome in his uniform?"

The woman—the last woman on earth he ever wanted to see—turned. What he was sure started as a smile when she heard his daughter's voice turned into a look of utter dismay. Had he not suddenly been filled with rage, the swift change of expressions would have been comical.

She had her nerve. First she'd returned to this town—his town. He could understand her need to attend her mother's funeral, but the service and burial were over. Clearly, she felt no need to be with her family if she'd spent even part of the day here. So why hadn't she left town? He didn't know, but he was going to find out. And then he was going to make sure she knew she wasn't welcome in Sweet Briar.

Robyn was oblivious to the tension. His little girl exhibited quite a bit of strength as she tugged his arm and led him in the woman's direction. He didn't want to talk to her any more than she wanted to talk to him, but he didn't want to hurt Robyn's feelings. Besides, he needed to know when she was leaving.

"Chief." She nervously clasped and unclasped her hands. Then she dropped her arms to her sides. Before he could speak, she folded her arms over her perfect breasts. As if suddenly aware that she looked defensive standing that way, she let her hands fall to her sides again.

"Miss Shields. I had no idea you'd still be in town." He managed to convey his dissatisfaction with her presence without raising his voice.

Alyssa, who'd been leaning against the door and sighing loudly at regular intervals, suddenly stepped into the room. Robyn might be too young to read body language or pick up on tones of voice, but Alyssa was a pro. Her interest piqued, she moved closer and looked from him to Carmen Shields. *Great.*

Carmen's brown eyes darted from him to his daughters and back. "I'm staying for a while."

Her voice was calm. Almost pleasant. But the years he'd spent in law enforcement had him noticing the way her pulse pounded at her throat, a clear indication of just how nervous she was. Good. He didn't want her to be comfortable.

What was it about Carmen Shields? He hadn't noticed

a woman since Anna's death. So why was the room suddenly so hot? And why was the blood suddenly pounding in *his* veins? The awareness he felt made him even angrier.

"How long is a while?" His voice wasn't pleasant and she flinched. He squelched the guilt that whispered in his ear to be nice.

"Are you asking as chief of police, or is this personal?"

His jaw tightened. Silence as a tactic generally worked.

She shrugged. "I'm staying two weeks."

"That's a long time. Don't you have to get back to your home?" He knew from her driver's license that she lived in New York City. The wild child had found a place fast enough to suit her.

"No."

"Goody. Then you can come to our house for dinner tonight. Right, Daddy?" Robyn asked, looking pleased.

The look of shock on Carmen Shields's face was priceless. He would have laughed if he didn't know he was wearing a similar expression.

"No," they spoke at the same time.

"Why not?" Robyn asked, looking between them.

"That's very nice of you, but I have plans. Thanks for thinking of me." Carmen glanced around the room as if searching for something to do with her hands, which were once again fluttering. Finding nothing left undone, she returned her attention to Trent and the girls. "Well, it's time for me to leave. I really enjoyed working with you, Robyn. I hope all of you have a nice evening."

She grabbed her purse and practically sprinted from the room.

"Bye, Miss Shields," Robyn called after her, and then turned her happy face to her father. "Isn't she nice? And pretty."

Alyssa, who had been quiet throughout the entire conversation, finally spoke. "Can we leave now?"

"Yes."

As Trent drove home, his stomach churned with anger. Carmen Shields had caused his family more than their share of tragedy. He wasn't going to stand still while she spent her days with his kids. He couldn't keep her from staying in Sweet Briar for two more weeks, but no way was she going to volunteer at the youth center, giving the kids of this town wild ideas. Not if he had anything to say about it. And as chief of police and a concerned parent, he most definitely did.

He made the drive home in record time, then started getting dinner ready. He shoved one of the endless casseroles Mrs. Watson had frozen before she left town into the microwave and set the timer. "Twenty minutes until dinner," he called to his daughters.

Snatching the phone from its base, Trent dialed Lex, his best friend and mayor of the town. Normally, he wouldn't go over Joni's head, but he couldn't take the risk that she would disagree with him. The center was always in need of help and she might not be willing to forbid that Shields woman from volunteering.

While the phone rang, Trent pulled a bag of packaged salad from the fridge. He ripped it open, removed a bowl from the cabinet and poured in the contents. Frowning at the lettuce and slivers of carrots, he grabbed a cucumber and a container of grape tomatoes.

"Devlin speaking."

"Lex. It's Trent. Got a minute?" He chopped the cucumber with more fervor than necessary and tossed the slices into the bowl. It wasn't the most exciting salad, but it was the best he could do.

"Sure. What's up?"

Trent opened the dishwasher and grabbed three clean plates and set them on the new pink-and-purple-checked place mats. The ones Anna had purchased years ago had faded over time. He couldn't find identical ones, but these were close.

"I need to talk to you about the youth center." Trent gathered up silverware and finished setting the kitchen table. "There's a woman volunteering who needs to be barred from the place."

"Shouldn't you be telling Joni?"

"I just found out." He pulled a couple bottles of salad dressing from the door of the refrigerator. Ranch for the girls and Italian for him.

"What's she done? Has she broken any laws?"

Trent frowned. "No. But she's not the kind of person who should be around impressionable kids."

"That's Joni's decision. She runs the center. If you're concerned about this woman, you need to let her know."

Trent grunted his dissatisfaction.

"You wouldn't like it if someone went over your head and tried to get rid of one of your officers. Show Joni the same respect."

Trent leaned against the counter. Lex was right. He'd resent the hell out of it if someone tried to do an end run around him. He'd do the fair thing and talk to Joni.

"Joni's probably going to call you, anyway."

"Why?"

Lex sighed and Trent knew that whatever it was, it wouldn't be something he wanted to hear. Thankfully, Lex never beat around the bush.

"Now that school is out, there'll be more opportunities for the teenagers to get into trouble."

Trent rubbed his hands across the back of his neck, squeezing it in a futile attempt to massage away the tension that had moved in seven years ago and been present every day since.

"That could lead to an adversarial relationship with your department, which is something we want to avoid," Lex continued. "Not to sound like a public service announcement, but we want our police department to have a good relationship with the youth of this town."

Trent was pretty sure he knew where this was leading, and he was definitely sure he wasn't going to like where they arrived.

"So I talked to Joni about you volunteering at the center. Naturally, she agreed."

"Naturally."

Lex ignored Trent's sarcasm. "Joni said there's a New York artist in town who's offered to create murals for the center. It'll take a couple of days for her to work up some sketches, so we've set up a meeting for later this week. I want you to pitch in on the murals. It'll give you an opportunity to interact with the teens outside of law enforcement."

Trent gritted his teeth. There couldn't be two women from New York visiting this small North Carolina town. Lex had to be talking about Carmen Shields. There was no way he could be around Carmen Shields for any length of time and keep his sanity.

"Playing Officer Friendly isn't my strength." That was the understatement of the decade. While he loved the younger kids, he had little patience for teenagers and their antics. "I'll assign one of my officers to work with them."

"Not an officer. You. You're the chief of police. You set the tone for the department. This will give you a chance to build better relationships with the teens, which you need. You have to interact with them in a nonadversarial setting. If they become comfortable with you, they'll be more willing to approach you if they become aware of someone planning to do something stupid."

Lex didn't say it, but Trent knew his reputation was that of a hard-ass. He kept a tight rein on the kids, keeping them on the straight and narrow. He and his officers wrote tickets to any driver exceeding the speed limit by even one mile. The curfew was enforced to the minute. Anyone caught drinking and driving was arrested.

Trent wasn't popular with the teenagers, but he kept his town safe. They might not appreciate it now, but he was protecting their futures. If kids used his picture for target practice, so be it. He'd do anything in his power to prevent another child from growing up without a mother. Anything except hang out with Carmen Shields.

Trent exhaled deeply. "How much time are we talking?"

"Not much. Just a few hours over a couple of days."

"Do I have a choice?" Trent rolled his shoulders, but the pain remained in his neck.

Lex laughed. "You always have a choice."

Sure he did. And pigs were circling his backyard, looking for a place to land. "I'll call Joni tonight and set it up."

Trent held the phone in his hand long after they'd said goodbye. There was no way he could work with Carmen Shields. He needed to run her out of town more than ever.

Chapter Seven

Carmen checked her sketches one last time before placing them in her portfolio. She'd spent the past two nights completing them. Once she started drawing, ideas had come one after the other until she could barely keep up. When she was finished, she had three options each for the various rooms, as well as the exterior of the building. The drawings for the exterior were the most daring.

If the center looked cool, maybe the cooler kids and those trying to be would be more inclined to participate in organized activities, as opposed to hanging around the beach and getting into trouble.

Joni had gotten the mayor's approval to paint the murals. Now they just needed to select the ones to be painted. That was the only item on the agenda for this morning's meeting. Carmen thought graffiti art would be fun for the kids and definitely give off a hip vibe. Of course, she had tamer options just in case Joni and the mayor didn't agree.

She got out of her car, ran her hands over her gauzy orange print skirt and headed for city hall. Joni had assured her that Mayor Devlin didn't let other people sway his thinking and wouldn't hold a youthful mistake against her. Carmen hoped Joni was right. Even though she'd be in town for only ten more days and didn't expect to interact with him much, it would be nice if he wasn't biased against her. Heaven knew she could use something good in her life right about now.

She closed her eyes against the rush of tears that threatened to spill over and ruin the makeup she'd so carefully applied. Her attempts to speak with her father had failed miserably. He'd swatted her away like a pesky fly buzzing around his picnic table.

He still wouldn't answer the phone, leaving that to Charlotte, who'd coolly told Carmen he wasn't taking calls. As if she were a mere acquaintance. She'd harbored a small hope that after seven years he regretted disowning her, or at least would forgive her. Each day that hope slipped away like sand in an hourglass, until only a few grains remained. If she hadn't committed to making amends to Anna Knight's family, she would've caught the first plane back to New York.

Although the chief did not want her to interact with his children, Robyn regularly sought her out. Carmen wanted to respect his wishes, but she couldn't reject the little girl and hurt her feelings. Robyn was a happy child who longed for a mother and repeatedly dropped hints about Carmen taking on that role. Ice had a better chance in hell than that happening.

Alyssa was the one who worried her. Sadness rolled off her in waves. Carmen had seen her at the youth center only a couple times, but each time she'd been miserable. And alone. Carmen hadn't yet found a way to reach her, but she wouldn't give up. Carmen knew from experience that a sad teenage girl could act out of desperation and make regrettable mistakes.

City hall hadn't changed. The two-story redbrick building with windows trimmed with white paint and white shutters at the end of Main Street had screamed small town to a girl longing for the excitement of a big city. Now, though, with its familiar black iron benches and potted plants on either side of the double doors, Sweet Briar City Hall felt like home.

She checked her watch. She was five minutes early. Promptness was a virtue that had been drilled into her from a young age. She hadn't appreciated the constant nagging then, but as a businesswoman, she understood the importance of showing others she valued their time.

Stepping inside, Carmen took a look around. Nothing had changed here, either. The walls were still a dull gray and the lighting still poor. No doubt the metal water fountain between the washrooms still didn't shoot higher than one inch no matter how hard you turned the knob. She passed wood doors with gold lettering identifying the water department, streets and sanitation and a few other city departments before reaching the double glass doors leading to the mayor's office.

She opened the door and nearly squealed with joy to see Denise Harper, the mayor's secretary. Mrs. Harper was one of the few people in town who'd ever stood up to Carmen's father. More important, she'd been fond of Carmen and always had a kind word and a smile for her.

"Is that you, Carmen?" Mrs. Harper asked, racing around her oversize desk to squeeze Carmen in a tight, breath-stealing hug. She rocked her from side to side before holding her at arm's length. "Just look at you. You're all grown up. And just as beautiful as I knew you'd be.

Seeing you is an answer to my prayers." She hugged Carmen tight again.

"I'm glad to see you, too." This warm reception almost took away the sting of her family's chilly treatment.

Mrs. Harper squeezed Carmen's hands. "I'm sorry about your mother. She was a good woman. And she did love you."

Carmen nodded, her heart in her throat. "Thanks."

"You need to get into your meeting. Let's have lunch one day this week and catch up on the past seven years."

"I'd like that."

Carmen followed the older woman down a short hall. Mrs. Harper knocked on the door, announced Carmen and then winked as she stepped aside to let Carmen enter the room. A warm feeling filled her as she realized that she did indeed have friends in town. Confirming that thought, her new friend Joni gave her a little wave from where she was standing beside a large credenza.

"Miss Shields, so glad you could join us."

Carmen followed the sound of the deep voice and came face-to-face with a stunningly handsome man. Here was something that had changed about city hall: this mayor looked a whole lot better than the previous one. She studied him with an artist's eye, cataloging his attributes. He was a couple inches over six feet, with coffee-colored skin, broad shoulders and a trim waist. Gray was sprinkled through his curly black hair. She guessed he was around forty.

Mayor Devlin didn't come close to her image of a small-town mayor. Sure, his tailored navy suit, white shirt and conservative red tie were appropriate for the job, but the mischievous twinkle in his eyes didn't fit. His charming smile made him seem more like a playboy. The nice kind with a heart, if there was such a thing.

She shook his hand and felt nothing. No spark. No

tingling. Nothing. Life would be too easy if she was attracted to this friendly man instead of the one who would like nothing more than to run her out of town, erect an electric fence around its borders and keep her out forever. But then, when had her life ever been easy?

"Help yourself to some refreshments. I realize it's early, but this is the only time I had free today."

"I'm just grateful we're not meeting at six," Joni quipped.

"I only schedule meetings at the crack of dawn when I expect to have a fight on my hands." The mayor grinned at Carmen. "Nothing helps people agree to be reasonable like a meeting held before the sun rises."

Carmen laughed. She joined Joni at the credenza, where she poured herself a mug of coffee from the silver-plated pot. She snagged an apple Danish and a napkin, then settled into a chair at the long table beside her friend. Mayor Devlin was seated at the head of the table, but he didn't appear anxious to get started.

He must have sensed her confusion. "We're waiting for one more person, then we'll begin."

"I'm not sure what I'm supposed to call you. Mr. Mayor? Or maybe you prefer Mayor Devlin?"

He aimed a killer smile at her and leaned back in his chair, folding his hands across his flat stomach. She bet he had a six-pack. "I prefer Your Highness or Your Majesty, but I can't get anyone to call me either of those. He-who-must-be-obeyed has a nice ring to it, but it just hasn't caught on."

She laughed. He was definitely different from Mayor Dooley, who hadn't had the slightest sense of humor. The old mayor must have believed the only thing keeping the earth in its orbit was the constant scowl on his face. Or maybe he'd just needed more fiber in his diet.

"I call him Mayor Nutcase," Joni pointed out, "but he refuses to answer to that. I can't figure out why."

The mayor laughed again. "Ignore her. I do." He looked at Joni, then shook his head as she stuck her tongue out at him. "Seriously, I don't stand much on formality. Just call me Lex."

Joni chimed in. "Short for Alexander Devlin III."

"Not to be confused with Alexander who is my grandfather and Alex who is my father." He took a swallow of his coffee. "We seem to lose letters with each generation. I guess I'll have to call my son L."

"How old is he?" Carmen asked.

"Who?"

"Your son."

He raised his hands, palms out. "I don't have a son. I'm not married. I'm not even dating anyone."

Joni rolled her eyes. "Neither subtle nor smooth, my brother."

Lex glanced at his watch. "I guess we should go ahead and begin. Trent must have gotten held up. I'll catch him up later."

Carmen choked on her Danish and her eyes watered. Chief Knight was coming to this meeting? Why? What could he possibly have to do with the youth center? She'd been there a couple of days and hadn't seen him since that first night, when he'd picked up his daughters and let her know he didn't want her in his town. Since then, he'd also let Joni know he didn't want Carmen near his daughters, but Joni had refused to be the bad guy. If he didn't want his daughters around Carmen, he would have to be the one to tell them.

"Are you okay?" Joni asked.

"I'm fine. I just swallowed wrong." She took a long drink of her coffee and hoped the meeting would end before the chief arrived.

"Then how about you show us the drawings," Lex suggested.

"Sure." She was pulling her sketches out of her portfolio when the door swung open. She didn't need to look up to know who had entered. The subtle change in the oxygen level, coupled with the sudden goose bumps that rose on her arms, let her know that Trenton Knight was in the building.

"Sorry I'm late," he said, closing the door behind him.

"No worries. We were just getting started. Grab a cup of coffee." Lex waved his hand in the general direction of the refreshments. "Have you met Miss Shields?"

"Yes." The frost in Chief Knight's one-word response brought the temperature in the room down to near Arctic levels.

Lex raised his eyebrows and looked from the chief to Carmen. Hadn't anyone informed the mayor how much the chief disliked her and that he blamed her for his wife's death? She wondered if the mayor would be as friendly to her when he found out.

Chief Knight stalked to the coffeepot and poured a cup. His muscles bunched under his shirt with each jerky movement. He didn't bother with cream or sugar. Carmen wondered if he was too angry to add sweeteners or if he really did prefer his coffee black.

After he took a seat, Carmen stood and placed her drawings on the easel the mayor provided. As an artist, she rarely did much public speaking. Her work spoke for her. She wasn't particularly uncomfortable speaking in front of people, but Chief Knight's presence had her nerves jangling like wind chimes in a tornado.

After she straightened her first sketch, she stepped aside so that the others could view it. When they turned their attention back to her, she spoke. To her dismay her voice didn't sound quite as confident as she would have liked.

"I thought this mural would be good for the exterior. It's one continuous scene that wraps around the building." She pointed to the dotted lines that marked the corner of each wall. "This shows kids of all ages participating in the different activities the center offers. The colors I have chosen can be changed if they are too bold. I have a smaller version of this picture in more subdued tones."

Bold colors were part of her signature, but she was willing to tone them down if they wanted her to. After all, the mural was for them, not her.

"That looks like graffiti," Chief Knight said, pointing an accusing finger at the sketch. His four words spoke an entire paragraph of disapproval.

"Graffiti art," Carmen corrected gently. "The majority of the mural will be painted with brushes. Graffiti art will be sprayed over it in places. There will also be a large section that is purely graffiti art."

"I arrest people who spray graffiti around the town. And you want to have them ruin the youth center and call it art. Not in my town."

"It is art," Carmen said, with a little more emphasis. "This isn't illegal. We aren't tagging private property without permission. It's a legitimate art form and kids are drawn to it."

She agreed that unauthorized graffiti was wrong even if some taggers showed unbelievable skill and imagination. But she'd spoken with one of the teenage boys at the youth center about graffiti art just the other day. He'd been aloof and disinterested until that conversation. The next morning he'd shown her some of his drawings. She'd incorporated graffiti art in the mural so that people like him could showcase their talent without destroying others' property.

"That trash might be considered art in New York, but

not here in Sweet Briar. But then, many things that are welcome in New York aren't wanted here."

"Trent," Joni gasped.

"Never mind," Carmen said, grabbing her work. "I was just trying to help. If the town isn't interested, that's fine with me."

"Hold on," Lex said, standing. "Let's take a look at the sketches. We can make changes to things we might not like, correct?"

"Yes. That was the purpose of this meeting."

"Then let's look at all of the drawings first and make decisions later. Agreed?" He looked meaningfully at Trent, who glared back and nodded curtly.

Joni rose and approached the easel. "I don't know about anyone else, but I think this is amazing."

"Thanks."

"It's graffiti," the chief repeated flatly, as if anyone was in doubt about his opinion.

"Do you really think we can do something like this?" Joni asked, ignoring Chief Knight.

"Sure. First the building needs to be primed. Then I'll sketch the design on the building. After that, it'll be like painting by numbers. And if you would prefer something a little tamer, I have that, too." She flipped to the drawings of more typical murals, without the graffiti.

Joni sighed and rubbed a perfectly manicured finger over the drawing. "Everything is so perfect. We're a group of amateurs. What if someone messes up? You know, what if someone paints with the wrong color?"

"No biggie. We can just paint over it. There are no mistakes that can't be fixed."

"I beg to differ." Trent's eyes were cold as ice, yet somehow they managed to incinerate her soul. "Of course, I'm not surprised someone like you thinks that."

Carmen knew some mistakes were irreversible. She'd lived with survivor's guilt for seven long years. She had lived while the others died. The fact that she hadn't been driving that night hadn't changed her feelings. Now she had the added burden of knowing an innocent woman had died, as well. Nothing she did would change that.

"Someone like me?" The words came out even though she didn't want to hear what he thought of her.

"Yes. Someone who destroys others' lives and then runs away. Someone who doesn't give a thought to the carnage they leave behind. It's easy to believe that mistakes can be glossed over when you aren't the one who has to suffer the consequences."

"Trent," Joni began, but Carmen stopped her with a hand on the arm.

"No. He's right. Some mistakes can never be erased. I know from personal experience. All a person can do is try to repair the damage they've done."

Carmen looked at Lex. "I'll leave my drawings here for you to look over. If you want to use them, let me know. If not..." She shrugged.

Lex clamped his jaw shut, as if locking words inside his mouth. After a moment of struggle, he spoke. "Leave your number with Mrs. Harper and I'll call you later."

Carmen didn't trust herself to speak, so she nodded and let herself out. For a minute she considered just getting in her car and driving, but where would she go? She knew that making amends wouldn't be easy. She just hadn't expected it to hurt so badly.

"I hope you're pleased with yourself, Trenton Knight," Joni said, an uncharacteristic frown on her face. "Carmen was only trying to help and you treated her like a criminal."

"Joni."

"Don't say a word to me. I don't want to hear anything you have to say." Joni spun to Lex. "I prefer the examples with the graffiti. I think the kids will really like it. Call me when you make your final decision."

"Joni," Trent repeated, but she ignored him. She grabbed her purse and stormed from the room, slamming the door behind her.

"Well, that was ugly," Lex said.

Trent snorted. "I never figured Joni for melodrama."

"I wasn't talking about Joni." The mayor huffed out a breath. "You want to talk about it?"

"No." Trent pushed to his feet, eager to get out of the room. Even though Carmen Shields was no longer around, the scent of her delicate perfume lingered in the air like an irritant, making him long for something he would never have again. That unwanted feeling was like tossing gasoline on his already burning anger and resentment. Fury threatened to consume him. She was the last woman he would ever want. "I've got to get back."

"I'm sure the officers can handle the safety of our fair city without you for another ten minutes." Lex waved Trent back into his seat and then poured more coffee into his own cup. "So what's going on between you and Carmen?"

"Oh, it's Carmen now, is it? Aren't you friendly." Hearing his best friend use her given name felt like a betrayal.

"Don't change the subject. You were pretty hostile to her."

"Nothing she doesn't deserve." Even as the words tumbled out of his mouth, Trent wondered if they were totally true. Carmen Shields may not deserve his friendship, but it didn't give him the right to treat her with contempt. He despised cruel men and he'd never deliberately hurt anyone. Until now.

Lex's eyebrows rose in surprise. "I'm lost here. She's only been in town for a couple of days. How has she managed to offend you in that short time?"

Now it was Trent's turn to be shocked. "Are you kidding me?"

"Do I sound like I'm kidding?"

"Don't you know who she is?"

"Should I?"

"She's the youngest Shields daughter." He closed his eyes in an effort to contain the fury and pain that erupted each time he thought of the accident. "She's the one responsible for Anna's death."

"I thought Dave Henry's son was driving. The way I heard it, he and another kid were drunk out of their minds and he blew through a stop sign." Lex looked at Trent as if awaiting confirmation.

Trent nodded. "She was with them. As the only survivor and witness, she should have been able to explain what happened, but she didn't. She conveniently left town after she gave only the barest statement in the coroner's inquest." He'd read the transcript of her testimony more times than he could count, looking for something to explain why he'd lost his Anna.

"I'm missing something here. How is she to blame? She wasn't even driving and they were all drunk."

"Carmen Shields was stone sober. She hadn't swallowed a drop of alcohol, but she didn't do anything to keep that idiot from driving."

Lex leaned forward in his chair. "She's young. She was even younger then. What was she, fifteen, maybe sixteen when the accident occurred? She didn't have the judgment that adults have."

"She was eighteen. That's old enough to vote and join the military. It's old enough to get married."

"Look, man, I know you're in pain. What happened to Anna was tragic in every sense of the word. But you're blaming the wrong person."

Trent slammed his mug on the table, sending coffee sloshing over the sides. He ignored the mess. "It isn't what she did. It's what she failed to do. She should have driven or taken his car keys. She should have done something. But she did nothing and my Anna died."

A tense silence hung over the room.

"You have to let it go," Lex finally said. "You can't be so hostile to her."

"Is that your opinion as my friend or an order from my boss?"

Lex wiped a hand down his face. "I'm not going to dignify that remark with an answer. I know better than anyone how much you loved Anna. She was a good woman. A great woman. But she's gone. And you have to let her go. You have to let go of the anger."

"Just like that." Trent snapped his fingers. "You expect me to just forget the woman I loved all my life. I'm not like you. I can't just wake up one morning and decide the woman I married doesn't matter to me. I can't forget what we shared." Lex flinched and Trent knew he was being unfair, but he was too angry to care.

"So you want to throw my marriage in my face?"

"Lex, I—"

"No. Don't backtrack now. Tell me, just what would you have done if Anna said she didn't want you anymore? Would you fight and hold on to her, or would you let her go so she could be happy? Of course, with your perfect marriage, you didn't have to deal with that. But don't think it's because you're so much better than us regular guys. It's because you got lucky with Anna."

"Lucky. My wife was killed in the prime of her life, and you think I'm lucky?"

"That didn't come out right. I just mean that you were blessed to have found such a wonderful woman."

"Yeah. And now you're telling me to forget her."

"I'm not telling you to forget her. I'd never do that. Anna loved you. She'd want you to move on with your life. You can't pretend that she's on vacation or at the store. She's gone, man. She's gone. And she's never coming back."

Trent shot to his feet. "You think I don't know that? I live with that fact. Every. Single. Day."

Before Lex could respond, he went on. "Alyssa and Robyn are the only reason I get up every morning. Alyssa only has a few memories of Anna. Robyn has no memory of her at all. How is it fair for my girls to grow up without a mother? How is it fair for Anna to have missed so much?"

"I'm not saying it's fair. It isn't. I understand you want to keep her memory alive for your girls. But you've overdone it. Your house has become a shrine to her. Have you changed one thing in seven years?"

"Of course."

"Name one."

Trent's mind raced furiously to find an example. His resentment grew when nothing came to mind. "I don't see where any of this is relevant."

Lex rose and moved around the table until he stood beside Trent. "You have to let her go."

"Why? Because it will make my friends feel better about stabbing me in the back and siding with that woman?"

"Nobody is siding against you."

"Anna was my world and Carmen Shields stole her from me. And you just expect me to get over that and make nice with her. How am I supposed to do that?"

Lex placed a hand on his shoulder. "One step at a time.

You start by letting go of the anger. Hating Carmen isn't going to bring back Anna."

"The thought of that woman being around my girls is making me crazy."

"She's only going to be here for a couple of weeks."

"It didn't take a couple of weeks for her to wreck my life. Hell, it didn't take two minutes. And every time I turn around, there she is. At the youth center. Here. In my thoughts."

"Your thoughts?"

"I didn't mean that."

"I think you did. Maybe that's the problem. Maybe you're so upset because you're attracted to her."

"No way in hell," Trent insisted, ignoring the tiny voice inside that contradicted him.

Chapter Eight

Carmen slowed her pace as she neared the youth center. She inhaled deeply in an effort to get her anger under control. That Trent Knight was unbelievable. How dare he insult her art? Trash. He'd called it trash. She was one of the most sought-after artists in New York. She couldn't paint fast enough to satisfy the demand for her work. It certainly wasn't trash.

True, the murals she'd designed were not her typical style. Her work was young and fun, but she'd never incorporated graffiti. But to her, it fit the vibe of the youth center.

And he'd called it trash.

His opinion shouldn't matter—he was just a small-minded man who hated her guts—but it did. His words cut straight to her heart. Because she knew he wasn't just talking about her art. He thought she was trash.

If only he knew. Her art was all that had saved her these past seven years. Without it, she might not have survived the pain and guilt. Sometimes she wondered if she truly had overcome it.

"Hi, Miss Shields."

Carmen turned and smiled at the familiar group of eight-year-old girls coming in her direction. She jokingly referred to them as her fan club. She returned their welcoming hugs, noting that Robyn hugged her just a little bit tighter and held on a little bit longer than the others. Poor thing. She really needed a mother's love. But with that judgmental father of hers, Carmen couldn't imagine that happening.

"How are you ladies today?"

The girls giggled, pleased to be addressed as ladies.

"Good. We can't wait for art. What are we making today?"

"Self-portraits. Using chalk." Carmen had spent the night planning the project and was anxious to see the kids' reactions. She smiled at each of the children. "Give me a few minutes to set up, okay?"

"Okay," the girls agreed, and then skipped away.

As Carmen headed toward the art room, she noticed a lone figure hunched in a chair in the game room, pulled far away from where three other teens were gathered. The trio leaned their heads together and talked quietly, although they frequently looked at the isolated girl and laughed. It didn't take a genius to figure out she was being deliberately excluded.

Carmen looked at the solitary girl and stifled a groan. It was the chief's daughter Alyssa. Carmen hesitated. She knew Chief Knight didn't want her interacting with his children. He didn't want her in the same town with them. But Carmen couldn't walk away from a child who was clearly in pain. Praying for guidance, she approached Alyssa. "Hi."

Alyssa looked at Carmen before turning her attention to the three whispering girls. "Hi."

"Remember me? I'm Carmen Shields."

"I know. We saw you at my mom's grave. And you teach art here. Robyn is always talking about you. It drives my dad crazy."

There was a burst of laughter and Alyssa flinched. Carmen sympathized instantly. She knew how it hurt to be an outsider.

"What are you reading?"

Alyssa turned the book so Carmen could see the front. It was a bestseller, but judging from the way Alyssa kept glancing at the group of girls, Carmen knew she would much rather be socializing than reading.

"I heard that was really good."

Alyssa nodded.

"If you get tired of reading, I have a great project in the art room."

"Art is for little kids like Robyn."

"Sure, they like it. But that's not what I had planned. I need help making examples of jewelry and fashion T-shirts for an older class. Any chance you might consider helping me?"

A spark of interest lit Alyssa's eyes. When she glanced at the other girls, that spark was extinguished. "I don't think so."

Carmen sat on a chair next to her. The girl's loneliness was screaming loud enough to break the sound barrier. "Well, if you change your mind, come on in. I'll have everything set up in about twenty minutes. Anytime after that will be fine."

"Sure," Alyssa murmured, not looking up.

Carmen had a feeling that Alyssa was agreeing just to get her to leave.

Helpless to do more, Carmen rose and crossed the room. A teenage boy stood in the doorway, his eyes focused on Alyssa and the other girls. Carmen wouldn't have noticed him at all if not for the intensity in his eyes. Fury shot from his every pore like flames.

He stepped in front of Carmen, blocking her path. "Are they still ignoring her?"

"It looks like it. Do you know why?"

"Yes." His voice was an angry hiss.

Carmen inclined her head, leading him down the hall so they wouldn't be overheard. "Why?"

He stared at her a minute, as if deciding whether or not to trust her. He leaned his head against the wall and expelled a breath. "Her father is the chief of police. A couple weeks ago, he broke up a party where kids were drinking. He called their parents and a lot of them got into trouble. Someone had the brilliant idea to get everyone to stop talking to her." He kicked his foot against the tile floor. "As if she had any control over her father."

"I see. Did those girls used to be friends of hers?"

He shrugged. "I don't know."

"Do you think it'll blow over?"

He shrugged again, but the worry in his eyes belied his nonchalance. He walked away, leaving Carmen alone with her thoughts. This was what Damon meant when he said that she needed to help the Knight family. She would find a way to help Alyssa before she made the same mistakes Carmen had made.

Trent walked into the office and took a handful of pink message slips from Ella, one of the three dispatchers. He sorted through them quickly.

"Good morning, Chief. Dr. Richards called from the

hospital. He said Mrs. Riley is awake and asking to speak with you this morning about the accident."

Damn. He'd hoped to have a minute of peace before the craziness of the day started. He rubbed his neck, trying to massage away the headache that had begun with his daily battle with Alyssa and gotten worse after his meeting about the mural.

Trent spun on his heels, heading for the door. "Let him know I'm on my way. And tell Officer Smith where I am if he needs me."

"Will do."

On the short ride to the hospital, Trent mentally reviewed the facts of the case. Bob Riley had suffered a fatal heart attack and driven his car into the lane of the 18-wheeler, setting off a chain reaction accident that injured nearly a dozen people. His wife, Tina, had been one of the casualties. Trent didn't need her statement at this moment, but he knew she needed to give it.

As Trent stood outside the hospital door, he scrambled to find the right words. In his experience, nothing anyone said could take away the agony that accompanied the death of a beloved mate. Meaningless platitudes had done nothing to diminish his grief. He'd barely understood anything that was said to him. If it hadn't been for his daughters, he would have crawled into a hole and died.

Trent knocked on the door and stepped into the room.

"Thanks for coming, Chief," Mrs. Riley said. Her head was bandaged and she had a cast on her right arm. Other than that, she looked okay. But there were tears in her eyes and a weary expression on her lined face.

"What's with the title? You've called me Trent all my life. Don't start chiefing me now."

She laughed and tears slipped down her cheek. "My Bob is gone."

"I know." Trent sat in the chair beside the bed and took her uninjured hand in his.

"Forty-three years. We were married forty-three wonderful years."

"He was a good man. One of the best I've known."

"Yes." She was silent with her thoughts, and he gave her the space she needed.

"I'm being released from the hospital this afternoon and leaving town after the funeral. I'm going to stay with my daughter Donna in Atlanta until my arm is better." Mrs. Riley gave a watery smile that nearly broke his heart. She was trying so hard to be brave, when he imagined she wanted to rail at God for the unfairness of it all.

"That's why I wanted to see you. I'm not sure when I'll be back. Or if I'll even come back." She swallowed and closed her eyes. "I heard a lot of people were hurt. I was hoping you would apologize to them for me. Let them know how sorry I am for my part in this." She shook her head, a mournful expression on her face.

"Your part? You were a passenger."

"I know." Her tears began to fall steadily. She didn't seem to notice them.

"Your husband had a heart attack and lost control of the vehicle. It was an accident, plain and simple. It wasn't his fault and it certainly wasn't yours."

"But it is my fault," she persisted, misery and guilt in every syllable. She looked at him as if pleading for his understanding. "Bob was my husband. I knew he didn't always eat right or get enough exercise."

"Everyone in town knew he was overweight. That doesn't mean we could have guessed he was going to have a heart attack. And neither could you. This was not your fault."

Trent pressed the call button for the nurse, then looked

directly into Mrs. Riley's eyes. "No one blames you. Please don't blame yourself."

The nurse rushed in, Donna and her brother, Doug, on her heels. Donna immediately sat on the edge of the bed and pulled her mother into her arms. Doug wiped his eyes, unashamed of the tears that streamed down his ruddy cheeks. Trent hoped they could find the words to help her let go of the guilt and find peace.

As he walked to the door, Trent patted Doug's shoulder. "Let me know if you need anything."

"Thanks. The only thing we need now is time to heal."

Trent nodded. He could have told Doug that time did only so much, but didn't. The other man would find out soon enough.

He hurried down the antiseptic-smelling hall, stepping around an abandoned wheelchair. No matter how fast he walked, he couldn't outrun the conversation with Tina Riley that was echoing in his head.

He knew people were responsible for their own actions. He'd always known that. So why had he blamed Carmen for Anna's death? She hadn't been driving the car that struck Anna's vehicle, yet he'd held her responsible for all these years.

That's not the same, he silently argued back. Carmen had hung out with troublemakers. She'd known the Henry kid had been drinking, yet she'd let him drive. Mrs. Riley had no idea her husband would have a heart attack. She was a responsible woman and never would have let her husband drive if she'd known he'd cause an accident.

Trent's stomach churned and he stopped walking, then leaned against the cotton-candy-pink wall. That was the very same thing Carmen had told him. If she'd known that Henry kid was going to crash, she wouldn't have let him drive. Unless she'd had a death wish at eighteen, that was the truth. After all, she'd gotten into the car with him, unknowingly putting her own life at risk.

Maybe Carmen wasn't entirely responsible for the accident that killed Anna. She hadn't been driving. Still, he wasn't yet ready to exonerate her. Knowing intellectually that Carmen hadn't caused the accident didn't change his feelings. She could have done something to prevent it. Perhaps one day he would feel differently, but for now his head and his heart were at odds.

Chapter Nine

Carmen stared at the darkening sky. It seemed like only a moment ago the sun was setting in all its red-and-orange glory. Now the sky was a beautiful indigo and the stars were battling to see which one would light up first. A soft breeze blew fresh ocean air and she inhaled deeply. She'd missed the salty fresh smell. She wiggled her toes in the still-warm sand, listening as the waves rolled up on the shore.

She stared at a star and then closed her eyes and, as she often had as a child, whispered the familiar rhyme. "Star light, star bright, first star I see tonight. I wish I may, I wish I might, have the wish I wish tonight."

Yeah, like that would work.

How many times had she wished to stay up past her bedtime, only to be hustled off to bed? Or for an extra piece of dessert? Too many. She could count on one hand the times her wishes had come true. Her father was inflexible when it came to rules, no matter how unimportant.

Would it have hurt anything for her to have had two pieces of chocolate cake once in a while? Especially since she'd always eaten her vegetables.

Foolish though she knew it was, she still made a wish, not daring to whisper it, but rather keeping it inside her heart. Maybe this time her wish would come true and she would be forgiven.

"You know, it's not wise for a woman to be alone on the beach at night."

Carmen jumped, then turned to find Chief Knight standing near her. She hadn't heard him approach. She attributed her rapidly beating heart to the fright and not to the attractive man close enough to touch.

Rather than stare at his utterly handsome face, she turned to look down the moonlit beach. In the distance she could see a couple strolling hand in hand on the edge of the incoming surf. "It's not that late. Besides, what do you care if someone harms me? No doubt you'd create a new holiday and have a parade if someone did me in. Then I'd be out of your hair permanently."

"That would ruin my crime statistics. Not to mention the paperwork involved. I loathe paperwork."

His voice was so flat she wasn't sure if he was serious. He certainly didn't seem the type to make jokes of any kind, especially not with her.

"Did you walk?"

She nodded.

"Come on. I'll walk you back to your father's house. I'm surprised he let you come out here alone."

"First off, I'm not staying with my father. I'm staying at the Sunrise B and B. Second, my father couldn't care less what I do."

She reached down and grabbed her sandals, looped them over her fingers and started toward the entrance to the beach. She'd strap them back on when she reached the sidewalk. Now that the chief had disturbed her tranquility, she saw no reason to remain. Even if he left, which he showed no sign of doing, she wouldn't be able to regain the peace she craved.

He walked beside her, shortening his stride to match hers. "Why aren't you staying with your father?"

She quickened her pace, her feet slipping and sliding in the sand. Why couldn't he just leave her alone? He'd already ruined her night. Wasn't that enough for him? "Not that it's any of your business, but I'm not welcome in my father's home. Or in either of my sisters' homes, for that matter."

Her eyes began to burn with unshed tears and she blinked rapidly, determined not to cry in front of this man. He'd already humiliated her this morning by insulting her work. There was no way she'd give him the satisfaction of seeing her cry. She sped up, walking as quickly as the shifting sand allowed. It squished between her toes and stuck to her damp feet.

"Since when?" He reached out to take her hand. She moved away before he could make contact, and lost her footing. He grabbed her arm, steadying her before she fell.

She jerked her arm free, ordering her skin to quit tingling from his touch. She wouldn't be attracted to this man. She wouldn't.

The moonlight illuminated his face. His eyes were so dark and intense she would find them beautiful on anyone else. On him, they were just cold and judgmental. Condemning. "Are you mocking me?"

"No."

"I haven't been inside that house since he threw me out seven years ago. Right after the coroner's inquest for my friends." Her father had used his influence to have the inquest conducted in record time. Once all the legalities were completed, he'd washed his hands of her.

The words he'd said that night were branded on her soul. *You brought shame on our family, Carmen Taylor. You're not worthy of the name Shields. If you want to be wild, do it somewhere else. You're no longer welcome here.*

His face hard as granite, he'd grabbed her by the elbow and lifted her off the couch. In one smooth motion, he'd opened the front door, pushed her out and closed it softly behind her.

Banished.

She turned and started across the beach, her shame made worse because she'd shared it with the chief. He reached a hand out to stop her progress, then clearly thought better of it. Instead, he stepped in front of her, effectively preventing her from walking away.

"Are you telling the truth?"

The shock in his voice startled her. He was standing so close she could feel the heat radiating from his body. He seemed troubled, although she couldn't imagine why. "Why would I lie about something like that?"

"He threw you out?"

"Yes."

He had the oddest expression on his face. She wasn't sure if she was reading him right, but he looked confused. That couldn't be right. It must be the play of shadows on his face.

"What? Why do you care, anyway?"

"I didn't know that's what happened. I thought..." He shook his head again.

Despite telling herself that she didn't care what he thought, she asked, "You thought what?"

"I thought your parents hustled you out of town so you wouldn't have to face the consequences of your actions."

Carmen laughed harshly. "Not hardly. My dad threw me out on my ear because I did the unforgivable. I brought shame upon the family. His exact words were no one in our family had ever seen the backseat of a police car. Until me."

She tried to blink back the tears in her eyes, but they fell anyway. She started to wipe them away, then changed her mind. Who cared if the chief saw her cry? He didn't matter to her. He was just one more inflexible man in the world who believed mistakes were things other people made.

"When I got home from making my statement, he told me just how ashamed he was of me. He was tired of cleaning up my messes. Since I couldn't conduct myself in a manner that lived up to the Shields name, I had to leave. He wouldn't even let me say goodbye to my mother." Carmen's voice cracked, but she refused to let it break. "He had one of his employees drive me to the bus station. Apparently, I couldn't even live in his town. I haven't seen or heard from my family in seven years. My sisters spoke to me after the graveside service, but only to let me know I hadn't been missed."

"God." Chief Knight squeezed the back of his neck, then shook his head.

She gulped and forced her voice past the huge lump that had suddenly appeared in her throat, making it difficult to speak above a pained whisper. "I had to read about my mother's death in the newspaper. If I hadn't seen the obituary, I wouldn't have had the chance to say a final goodbye to her. I didn't have the chance when she was alive."

Carmen wrapped her arms around her waist in an effort to hold herself together. Although the night was still warm, she felt cold. And empty. "My mother went to her room in tears when we got home from the inquest. Both of my sisters were at our house. They were standing there when my father put me out. They each had a place of their own, but neither of them offered to let me stay the night. So I left."

"I had no idea." The man who blamed her for his wife's death actually sounded pained, which didn't make sense. He should be doing handstands at the thought of her being forced out of her home with nowhere to go. At least nowhere safe.

"Why? Where did you think I was all this time?"

"I thought you were off living the good life, never giving the accident a second thought."

"No. Far from it." She'd been a scared kid cast out of her home with only a few dollars in her pockets. Instead of wasting money taking a bus to some random destination, she'd hitchhiked out of town that night. Fortunately for her, she'd met Damon shortly thereafter. He'd rescued her before her situation became too dire.

"And you might not believe it, but that accident has haunted me day and night for seven years. I still wake up screaming from nightmares. I didn't know your wife died, but I knew Donny and Jay did. I knew I was the only one riding in our car who walked away."

Physically, she'd been unhurt. Emotionally, she'd been destroyed. Seeing the devastation of the accident had been awful. Having her entire family turn against her had been catastrophic. She hadn't believed her family no longer cared for her. She still had a hard time with that bit of truth, although with each passing day she was coming to accept it.

Trent stood stock-still as a wide range of emotions pummeled his insides. Guilt battled with disbelief, while anger and shock wrestled for dominance. How could he have gotten it so wrong? How could he have not known the truth? The answer was simple: he hadn't wanted to know the truth.

He'd lost his precious Anna too soon and needed someone to blame. It hadn't been enough to blame the dead driver. The dead neither know nor care if you despise them with every fiber of your being. He'd needed a living, breathing target for his hostility, and Carmen had been it.

He looked into her eyes. There was a world of sorrow and pain beneath the shimmering tears. A lone tear leaked from her eye and slowly slid down her cheek.

Damn. He didn't want to feel sorry for her. Although the rational part of him now knew she wasn't to blame for Anna's death and that she had suffered as well, he didn't want to change his opinion of her. He was too used to casting her in the role of the villain to start thinking of her as a victim who'd lost as much as he had that night. Despite that, he did feel sorry for her.

He was disgusted with himself for noticing how lovely her eyes were. He'd never be able to drink a cup of coffee again without thinking of her eyes. That thought added to his annoyance.

He didn't like the way his body reacted to her nearness, to her incredible beauty. Her sweet scent. He couldn't stand the tenderness growing inside him. He didn't want to be attracted to her. In all honesty, he couldn't justify hating her, but he couldn't suddenly change his feelings to friendship or, God forbid, anything else.

Trent told himself to step aside so she could pass, but he didn't. Seeing a woman in tears always tore him up. Even if that woman was Carmen Shields.

He dug into his pocket, pulled out a handkerchief and offered it to her. She tilted her head in confusion before taking it and wiping her eyes.

"I'm sorry," he said.

"Don't be. I'm getting used to their rejection."

"That's not what I meant, although I'm sorry for the way your family is treating you."

She blinked at him again. "Then why are you apologizing?"

He realized he was standing close enough to inhale her scent and jerked back, shoving his hands into his pockets. "I'm sorry for blaming you for something that wasn't your fault. You weren't responsible for Anna's death. You weren't the driver. You were a passenger. An innocent bystander."

"I didn't try hard enough to stop Donny from driving. Maybe if I did something different, he might not have driven."

"Maybe. Maybe not." What difference did it make? She couldn't go back and take the keys. She could wonder all she wanted, but in the end his beloved Anna was still gone.

"Does this mean you don't still blame me?" Carmen was clearly holding her breath, the moon illuminating the hope shining in her eyes. Seeing how much his opinion mattered to her humbled him.

"I never should have held you responsible in the first place."

She released her breath in a soft sigh. "Thanks."

She smiled and his heart thumped in his chest and desire began to grow. But he couldn't betray Anna like that. Suddenly angry at his response, he snapped, "That doesn't mean we're friends, however. We're not. Nor will we ever be."

Carmen's smile disappeared and, in a blink, the light left her eyes. Seeing the change in her hurt him in a way he didn't quite understand and definitely didn't like.

"Don't worry, Chief. I would never mistake you for a friend. Now if you'll excuse me, I need to get back to my room." She brushed past him and hurried across the beach. When she reached the sidewalk, she stopped, put on her sandals and hurried down the street.

He sighed and followed her at a distance, watching until she reached the B and B. Once she was safely inside, he continued his rounds, trying to keep his mind blank. After he assured himself his town was secure for the night, he headed home.

Chapter Ten

Trent stared into his cup as if the coffee held magical power to solve his problems. He hadn't slept well the past few nights. The image of Carmen's sorrowful expression constantly haunted him whenever he closed his eyes. His guilt prodded him to be a better man, but he didn't know what that meant when it came to Carmen Shields.

To make matters worse, the mural was being painted today. Lex had made it clear he expected Trent to help out. Somehow Joni and Carmen had rounded up most of the town's teenagers and quite a few college kids to help paint. Trent had been outvoted and the mural would include graffiti. One of the worst teen taggers had been recruited to do the deed.

Trent drained his now lukewarm coffee and put his cup in the dishwasher. Rubbing his hands over a well-worn T-shirt, he called to the girls.

There was one good thing to come from this duty. He

would get to spend time with his daughters. Robyn had been thrilled when he'd told them he'd be helping paint the mural. She'd clapped her hands ecstatically and given him a big hug. Alyssa had been quiet, although he thought he detected a hint of enthusiasm in her eyes. Of course, with the way Alyssa's mood changed, she could hate the idea today.

"I'm ready, Daddy," Robyn called as she charged into the room, bumping into a table and sending a framed photo crashing to the floor. She picked it up, then pulled to a screeching halt in front of him. Even standing still she radiated motion.

"So I see." He was surprised that his little fashion plate was wearing plain denim shorts and an equally plain blue T-shirt. He didn't know she even had clothes without flowers or other designs. She certainly never wore them.

His thoughts must have shown on his face because she frowned down at her clothes. "Alyssa said even if I'm careful I might get paint on myself. I don't want to mess up any of my pretty clothes."

"Good thinking."

"I'm ready, too," Alyssa said from the bottom of the stairs. She was dressed similarly to Robyn, although her T-shirt was purple. Her hair was pulled back into a ponytail and she wore a purple baseball cap. She had a blue cap in her hand, which she put on her sister's head.

Robyn immediately pulled off the cap and gave it back to her sister. "I don't want to wear that. It'll mess up my hair." She ran her hands over her hair, then checked in a wall mirror to be sure every strand was in place.

"I know. But you don't want to get paint in your pretty hair, do you? Green and orange are nice for paintings, but you don't want orange hair."

Robyn hesitated a moment and then shook her head.

"So wear it."

Robyn gave a long-suffering sigh. "Okay. But only because I like my hair the color it is."

"So do I."

Robyn took the hat. "I'll wait until we get to the center to put it on."

Alyssa shook her head and grinned at Trent. He returned her smile and in that one instant knew perfect peace. It wouldn't last, but it had been a long time since he and Alyssa shared a nice father and daughter moment.

The ride to the center was enjoyable, although the closer they got, the quieter and more withdrawn Alyssa became. Even though she hadn't mentioned it again, he knew the other kids were still giving her a hard time. Maybe he'd been wrong and this thing wasn't going to blow over. Perhaps he should call some parents and let them know what their little darlings were up to.

But he knew he couldn't do that. Alyssa would be furious if he interfered in her life. Not only that, it would embarrass her in front of the other kids. Man, he hated not being able to help his child. He wished he had someone to discuss this with. Making all the decisions alone was stressful.

He pulled into a parking spot on the street. Alyssa squared her shoulders and exhaled loudly.

"Alyssa," he began, not sure what to say.

"I'll be all right." Her voice was soft but firm. His brave little warrior.

"You sure?"

"Yes. Carmen told me not to let the small-minded people get to me. It's hard not to have friends to hang out with, but Carmen lets me hang out with her. She's teaching me how to make jewelry. She's way cool. I want to help her with the mural."

Trent didn't like the idea of Alyssa hanging out with Carmen Shields no matter how cool she was, but his daughters hopped out of the car before he could voice his objection again.

He removed the keys and followed at a slower pace, surveying the area. Groups of teens were huddled in various sections of the parking lot, some laughing and others horsing around. He recognized quite a few kids from town. He was surprised to see a group of the wealthier kids from the homes on the golf course standing off by themselves. Their parents hadn't struck him as the type to want their children using the youth center.

He easily spotted Robyn in a cluster of giggling girls. They gave an ear-piercing squeal when another little girl broke away from her mother, running to join their group. Laughing and hugging, they jumped up and down. Hadn't they seen each other yesterday?

Alyssa was a little harder to spot. He scanned the groups of teens, hoping that Alyssa would be among them. She wasn't. She was standing alone by the tables of paint. He was making his way in that direction when a woman joined her. They embraced like old friends.

In less time than it took to inhale, he recognized Carmen Shields. Dressed in frayed shorts that revealed her trim legs and a plain army-green T-shirt that molded her every curve, she shouldn't have looked so enticing. Yet his body reacted as if she wore a tiny bikini. He forced himself to exhale and ordered his eyes to look away. They wouldn't obey.

Her wavy hair caught in a swirl of wind. She pulled an elastic band from her wrist and gathered her locks in a messy ponytail that looked sexier than it should have. Her T-shirt rose, revealing a strip of smooth café au lait skin.

The two chatted, Carmen's arm firmly around Alyssa's

shoulders. Alyssa gestured as she talked, looking more animated than he'd seen her in weeks, if not months. This was the daughter he missed.

"Yo, Trent." He turned and waited as Lex approached him. Like Trent and the other men present, the mayor wore jeans and an old T-shirt. "Glad you could make it."

"You issued such a friendly invitation, how could I refuse?"

Lex grinned. "Looks like a pretty good turnout, though we could use a few more adults."

"Unfortunately, that's too often the case. Most of the kids I deal with wouldn't get into so much trouble if they had active parents in their lives. Not that I accept that as an excuse to break the law."

"Of course not. Nothing is a good enough excuse for you."

Trent wasn't sure if that was an insult or just an astute observation. Either way, it was true.

Joni's voice came over a portable microphone. "Okay, we'd like to get started. Please gather around."

Everyone moved to the front of the building, where Joni stood on a makeshift stage. Trent stayed near the back, where he could keep his eyes on the crowd. "I'd like to thank all of you for coming," she said. "Fortunately, we have a beautiful sunny day for working outside."

A few people cheered.

"Mayor Devlin, would you like to say a few words?"

Lex shook his head and Trent smiled. That was one thing he admired about Lex. Unlike the former mayor, or politicians in general, Lex wasn't in love with the sound of his voice.

"Okay, then. We'll have a few words from our artist and get to work. Some of you may remember Carmen Shields. She grew up in Sweet Briar. What you may not know is that she is the famous artist Carmen Taylor. Without further ado, all the way from New York, I give you Carmen Taylor."

There was a smattering of applause and a couple calls of "Welcome home." Carmen stepped onto the stage beside Joni, took the microphone and glanced around. She bit her lip and tapped the fingers of her free hand against her thigh. Clearly, she didn't enjoy public speaking.

"I don't really know what to say. Thanks so much for helping to paint." There was a bit of laughter. "I've got pictures inside showing what each of the murals will look like when they're finished. Please feel free to check them out. Today we're only painting the outside of the building.

"As you can see, some wonderful volunteers have primed the walls. I've also sketched the outline of what we'll be painting today. You'll see numbers on the walls, too. They represent different colors and correspond to the numbers you'll see on the cans of paint. All you have to do is match them up."

"So we'll be painting by number?" someone called.

"Yes. Exactly."

"Even my brother can't mess that up," one teen yelled, to the amusement of the crowd.

Carmen laughed as well, a sweet sound that warmed Trent's blood.

A kid of about nine raised his hand. "What if someone makes a mistake and uses the wrong color?"

Carmen gnawed on her lip, suddenly looking uncertain. She met Trent's eyes and then hers skittered away. When Joni had asked that same question, Carmen had been ready with an answer. And he'd bitten her head off. Insulted her. Now, thanks to him, she didn't know what to say.

Guilt churned the contents of his stomach. Before he could think too much about his motives, he answered the boy's question. "There are no mistakes in art. If you use the wrong color, I'm sure Miss Shields can find a way to make it work."

Carmen gasped and surprise lit her face. He hoped she heard the apology in his voice. She smiled and the already bright day got even brighter. Their eyes met and something he recognized arced between them. Appreciation. And attraction.

"Chief Knight is right. Little mistakes will only make the mural more interesting. And artists love interesting. Let's just not make it too interesting."

The crowd laughed.

She looked around. "If there are no more questions, everyone grab a partner and let's get to work. Or I should say, let's go have fun."

There was an excited buzz as people rushed toward the table and grabbed paint, trays and brushes. Trent worried that Alyssa wouldn't have a partner. If she didn't object, he'd be her partner. It would give him a chance to work at restoring their relationship.

He spotted her on the edge of the crowd. He was almost to her when the mother of Robyn's best friend stopped him. She invited Robyn to spend the night with Juliet. Trent quickly accepted the invitation, then rushed away, promising to get the details later.

When he reached Alyssa, she was with Carmen. His daughter smiled at him. "Hey, Dad."

"Hey."

"Isn't this so cool? Have you seen Carmen's drawings? The murals are going to look so great. Especially with Joseph's art."

Trent held back a snort. It wasn't art. It was graffiti. Joseph Whitfield had tagged more than his share of buildings in and around Sweet Briar. True, he hadn't done any damage in a while, but Trent and his officers were keeping an eye on him.

Four girls Trent recognized as Alyssa's classmates stood nearby. They whispered behind their hands and then laughed. Alyssa's mouth tightened, but other than that she gave no outward sign she'd heard them. Good for her.

"Hey, Alyssa." A teenage boy walked past the giggling girls. Speak of the devil. It was Joseph Whitfield. "I heard you don't have a partner."

She raised her chin. "No."

He grinned. "Neither do I. Do you want to be my partner?"

Alyssa smiled brighter than Trent had ever seen. "Sure. If you want to."

"I do. I'm not sure how good I'll be with a paintbrush. I'm better with spray paint." Joseph moved to Alyssa's side, standing too close for Trent's comfort.

Trent clenched his jaw, holding back a streak of swearwords.

"Hi, Chief. It's nice to see you." The teen extended his hand. Trent paused before taking it, swallowing the urge to shove the kid away from his innocent daughter. "I want you to know that I haven't been tagging buildings. I won't be doing it again, either. Well, except for here. I'll be working on canvas from now on."

"That's good to know."

Joseph smiled at Alyssa again. "Come on. Most of the crowd is gone. Let's grab some paint and brushes."

Carmen watched the teens walk away with no small amount of satisfaction, then glanced over at Alyssa's dad. Chief Knight's jaw was clenched so tight his teeth had to be cracking. His eyes were fixed on Joseph and Alyssa, who were talking to a couple other teenagers.

"What's wrong?"

"I didn't know Alyssa and Joseph knew each other."

"Really? He's been very sweet to her. The other kids have been ostracizing her, but not him. He always speaks to her when he comes to the center. He's really a nice young man."

"*Man* being the operative word. He's way too old to be hanging around her."

"Too old? He's seventeen."

"Exactly. Alyssa is fourteen."

Carmen nearly swallowed her tongue. "Fourteen? I thought she was sixteen."

"No. She looks older than she is."

"I didn't know. She seemed so lonely. And Joseph was always so concerned about her. I encouraged him to befriend her."

Trent frowned and stared at Carmen, his black eyes hard. He flexed his hands several times as if trying to get his temper under control. When he spoke, it was through clenched teeth. "I wish you hadn't done that. Don't you think you should have asked me before setting my daughter up with some guy?"

She knew he wanted her to apologize, but she couldn't. Alyssa needed friends. Loneliness was a great catalyst for horrible decisions. Carmen knew that firsthand.

A quick glance revealed she and the chief were beginning to draw attention. She didn't want to have this discussion in front of an audience.

She tilted her head toward the center. "Let's take this inside."

"Fine."

They walked side by side, neither one speaking. He was so close she felt the heat rolling from his body. A volunteer with a dripping brush stepped into her path. Carmen automatically moved aside and bumped into Trent. She gasped and inhaled his clean, masculine scent and the hint of aftershave. Scolding herself for noticing how very male he was, she mumbled an apology and hurried inside.

She led the way to the art room, hoping the familiar surroundings and the comforting smell of paint would slow her rapidly beating heart.

He closed the door behind them, but the calm she hoped for didn't come. She still felt the thud of her heart and the blood rushing through her veins. She reminded herself she had no right to notice the way his massive chest expanded with every breath he took. If not for her, his wife would still be alive.

"You want to explain why you felt you had a right to set up my daughter?"

"I didn't set them up. I just suggested that Joseph be her friend. I don't see what the big deal is. Alyssa's going to be in high school in the fall, right?"

"What's your point?"

"Unless Sweet Briar High has grown significantly in the past seven years, they were bound to meet."

He shook his head. "You're unbelievable. You encourage my daughter to become friends with a criminal and justify it because they might pass in the hallway at school. Incredible."

He turned to walk away, but Carmen grabbed his arm. Electricity shot through her fingers and spread throughout her body. Dropping her hand, she forced herself to concentrate on the conversation and not the effect one simple touch had on her. "What are you talking about? Joseph isn't a criminal."

"Of course he is. He's sprayed graffiti on plenty of buildings and fences in this town."

"And?"

"And what?"

"Isn't this the part where you tell me he just got out of prison?"

Sarcasm was definitely a mistake.

Chief Knight's eyes narrowed until they were mere slits. "He didn't go to prison. Little punk wasn't even prosecuted. Unfortunately, bleeding hearts run the justice system."

"Or maybe they have compassion and aren't as eager to ruin a kid's life as other people may be. Maybe they see the promise in him. I do. He's really talented."

"Oh, well. The great Carmen Shields thinks he's talented. Let's all just ignore his criminal behavior." Trent snapped his fingers. "Just like that, his past disappears."

Although they were talking about Joseph, she couldn't help but think they were talking about her, as well. The chief's attitude hurt her even though she already knew he disliked her. "I'm not saying his past doesn't matter. But he has a great future."

"And you know this how? Did you see it in your crystal ball?"

"He showed me his drawings. He's really good."

"He still broke the law."

She wanted to shake this stubborn man. Of course, that wouldn't change his mind about Joseph. Or about her. How could a man with a body so perfect her fingers ached to paint it be so unyielding? She expelled a breath and softened her voice. "I understand that. He was young. Are you going to hold that mistake against him forever?" Would he hold her mistakes against her forever?

"His youth doesn't excuse breaking the law. Nothing does." Trent shook his head in disgust. "I'm wasting my time expecting understanding from someone like…" His voice died out.

"Don't stop now, Chief. Go ahead and finish. You don't

expect someone like me to understand. Someone lacking. Someone less than. My father always made sure I understood I wasn't worthy of the Shields name."

Now Chief Knight was judging her just as harshly. The pain was like a dagger plunged in her heart. His opinion shouldn't matter, but it did. She stepped back and spun away.

"Carmen."

She froze but didn't turn around. He'd never called her by her first name before. Despite how hurt she felt, hearing her name on his lips made her skin tingle.

"I'm sorry." His voice was husky. Pained.

She was surprised by his apology. Given the way she'd ripped apart his life, it was the last thing she expected. "I understand."

"Really? Then maybe you can explain it to me. I don't mean to say such horrible things to you, yet I can't seem to stop."

She looked at him and smiled sadly. "It's simple. You hate me."

He huffed out a breath. Clearly, he hadn't expected her candor. He shook his head slowly. "I don't hate you. I know you aren't to blame for Anna's death. You were in the wrong place at the wrong time."

"That's your head speaking. You heart still thinks it's my fault."

A hair had escaped from her ponytail. He brushed it behind her ear, letting his fingertips drift over her cheek. Trembles shook her and her knees weakened. Every nerve ending was on high alert.

She licked her lips and his eyes followed the path of her tongue. His nostrils flared even as his eyes narrowed. He stared at her mouth as if he wanted to kiss her. She had to be misinterpreting his actions. He couldn't possibly want to kiss someone like her.

He dropped his hand as if his fingers were singed, then took a giant step backward, building an invisible barrier between them.

She quashed her disappointment and longing, then steered the conversation back where it belonged. "If you want, I'll tell Joseph to stay away from Alyssa."

"After the way she looked at him, like he was her own personal hero, I don't think so. She'd only blame me. We don't need more tension in our relationship." Trent's shoulders slumped and he suddenly seemed exhausted. "But... I don't know. He's so much older. And his past bothers me. I have no idea what's right and what's wrong. I just don't want to mess up."

"Mess up what?"

"Alyssa."

He sounded so sad, Carmen's heart ached for him. She'd misjudged him. She'd painted him with the same brush as her father, deciding he was harsh and judgmental and unconcerned about his kids. Nothing could be further from the truth.

She sat at a table, then indicated a chair beside her, waiting until he sat before speaking. "Alyssa is a terrific girl. You're doing a great job with her."

"It's hard. I'm stumbling around in the dark. Most days she barely speaks to me."

"She's a teenage girl. A bad attitude comes with the territory. And she's been having a rough time of it lately."

"She'd begun shutting me out of her life long before any of this started." He rubbed his neck. Carmen wished she was brave enough to push his hands aside and massage away his tension, but she knew he didn't want her to touch him. So she curled her hands into fists and kept them in her lap. "I don't know what to do. If only Anna was here. She'd have the answer."

Carmen inhaled. She'd wondered about Anna for a while but hadn't dared mention her. "What was your wife like?"

"Wonderful. She was the best person I knew."

"How did you meet?"

He stretched his legs in front of him, letting his mind drift back in time. "Second day of sixth grade at Frederick Douglass Middle School. Her family moved here from Indiana. I can still picture her standing at the front of the room while Mrs. McGrath introduced her. She was tall and thin with long black beaded braids. I couldn't tear my eyes away. She was the most beautiful girl I had ever seen." He grinned, and Carmen easily envisioned him as a love-struck boy. "In those days, teachers had students sit in alphabetical order. I never understood why, but boy, was I glad."

"Why?"

"Anna's last name was Kingston. She sat next to me for three years. A lot of tall girls slump and try to look shorter. Not my Anna. She was proud of her height and stood erect like a queen."

He laughed, something Carmen couldn't recall ever hearing him do. The sound raised goose bumps on her arms and she wished he would laugh again.

"Unfortunately, I was short. I was shorter than all of the boys and most of the girls."

"You? But you're so tall."

"Now. I didn't reach five feet until freshman year of high school. It took two more years for me to reach six feet."

"Wow."

He nodded. "The difference in height made me skittish

for about five seconds. Until she sat next to me. She smiled and I was a goner. I fell in love that second and knew I'd love her for the rest of my life."

Carmen thought she saw his eyes well with tears before he closed them and pretended to rub tiredness away.

He cleared his throat, yet when he spoke his voice was husky. "She always claimed she'd loved me longer. She used to joke that she fell in love with me when she walked up to the desk and that's why she smiled. We knew from the start we would be together. We dated all through high school and got married right after college."

Without a doubt he'd loved his wife completely. That he'd lost her so soon was tragic. Carmen swallowed the lump in her throat and stifled the urge to reach out to him. Suddenly, the chief of police seemed alone and vulnerable.

"Anna is the only girl I ever loved. The only girl I ever kissed. The only woman I ever..." His voice faded as his thoughts wandered into private memories, making Carmen feel like a voyeur who had no right to hear any of this.

"You still miss her."

"With every breath I take."

Silence reigned for several long moments. Finally, he rapped his knuckles on the table and stood. "We should get back so you can keep an eye on the progress."

Though she longed to remain and bask in the comfort she felt with him, she nodded. "You're right."

Ever the gentleman, he pulled out her chair, then stood back to let her pass. As they joined the volunteers, she couldn't stop thinking about the way Trent loved Anna, and wishing someone would love her that way, too.

Chapter Eleven

Carmen walked around the youth center, picking up stray paintbrushes while surveying the mural. The volunteers had done a superior job of bringing her vision to life. True, there were places where lines were painted over, and spots where the paint was too thick, but overall, it was perfect.

Best was the fifteen-foot-wide area featuring Joseph's graffiti art. It was so vibrant. So fun. Even a couple grumpy old men passing by grudgingly admitted it livened up the mural. One even patted a beaming Joseph on the shoulder. Once the rest of the mural was dry, Joseph would add graffiti to several other areas to make them pop, as well.

"I thought I'd find you here. Why aren't you at the park getting something to eat?"

Upon hearing Joni's voice, Carmen glanced over her shoulder and smiled at the woman, who had become a good friend. Joni's brother had prepared lunch for the volunteers. "I wanted to touch up a few areas while the paint was still wet. It's easier that way. And there's always that odd brush that ends up on the ground that needs cleaning. I figured I'd finish here and head over in a few minutes."

"You obviously have never seen teenage boys eat. A pack of hungry wolves could take lessons from them. I doubt there's a hot dog bun left, much less a hot dog. And forget about ribs. They probably even ate the bones."

Carmen laughed. Her stomach growled; it wasn't nearly as amused.

Joni continued, "Lucky for you, you have a great friend. I risked life and limb to grab food before they devoured it all."

"I'm forever in your debt."

Joni looked at the painted wall and sobered. Her voice rang with sincerity. "You've got that backward. We owe you." She gestured with the foil-covered pan she was holding. "Wash your hands and let's eat while it's hot."

Ten minutes later they sat in the snack room, plates of ribs, potato salad, coleslaw and baked beans in front of them. Condensation rolled down the ice-cold cans of cola, forming rings on the laminate folding table.

Carmen bit into the tender meat and closed her eyes in pleasure. "I think I'm in love with your brother."

"You and every other woman in this town." Joni shrugged. "I don't see it."

"That's because he's your brother. But trust me, there's something about a man who can cook. Instant turn-on. Not to mention he's seriously hot."

"Would *eww* be an acceptable response here?"

Carmen laughed. "Only because you're his sister. Otherwise I'd suggest you get your eyes checked."

"Speaking of men, is everything okay between you and Trent?"

Carmen scooped some beans into her mouth, chewing slowly to stall. "Why do you ask?" she finally replied.

"I saw the two of you talking. Actually, it looked like you were arguing. Then you went inside. Is he still giving you a hard time about the mural?"

Carmen wiped her hands on her napkin. "No. He was a little worried about Joseph and Alyssa being partners."

Joni sipped her drink and then nodded. "Oh. That's understandable."

"What do you mean?"

"Don't go all mama grizzly on me. I'm not attacking Joseph. I like him. And I saw the way he and Alyssa were looking at each other. I just meant it must be hard on Trent, watching his little girl grow up before his eyes."

"I imagine it is."

"It has to be twice as hard for him as a single father. For both of them, really. Alyssa doesn't have a mother to help guide her. He does the best he can, but let's face it, a man doesn't know what it's like to be a teenage girl. And if there is a man without a feminine side, it's Trent Knight. He's practically a caveman." Joni bit into a rib for emphasis.

"Not a caveman, but definitely all man."

Joni placed her bone on the plate and took a sip of her soda. "Well, well. That sounds interesting. What were you guys doing in here?"

"Just talking. What else would we be doing? The man can barely stand to look at me."

"I wouldn't say that. I saw him checking out your, um, assets plenty of times today."

Carmen felt her cheeks heat. "We'll never be friends." He'd told her that himself.

"You know what they say about that thin line between love and hate?"

"That doesn't apply to Trent. He lives in a black-and-white, good-and-evil type of world. And you know where he puts me."

Joni frowned, but she didn't reply. There was nothing she could say.

"Anyway, it doesn't matter. I'm leaving tomorrow."

"I don't suppose there's anything I can say to change your mind."

"No. It's time for me to leave."

"Have you made any progress with your father or sisters?"

Carmen had broken down and confided in Joni about her estrangement from her family. "No. Daddy still refuses to see me. As long as he won't, they won't."

"I wish there was something I could do."

"There is."

"What?"

"Look after Alyssa for me. I know you care about all the kids, but she needs extra attention now."

"You really care about her."

Carmen nodded.

"Consider it done."

"I'm going to miss you."

"This isn't the end. I'm coming to visit you in the fall. Sooner if my brother can keep a waitress for more than a week. And you'll come back here."

"No. I'm never coming back." Carmen's heart ached at the thought of never seeing her hometown again, but her family's rejection hurt too much. "There's nothing for me here. When I leave Sweet Briar tomorrow, it'll be forever."

Trent stared at the framed photograph in his hands. Anna had never looked more beautiful than she did on their wedding day. Her always bright eyes had shone even more as she'd stared at him. He ran a finger over the glass, wishing, as he often did, to be able to touch his wife's skin just one more time. Instead, he felt only the cold, hard glass.

He set the picture back on the mantel and then stared at his hands. Only hours ago these fingers had caressed another woman's cheek. A woman he'd hated for years. True, he no longer believed she was responsible for the accident. But still. How could he have done that?

Although Anna was gone, Trent still felt guilty. The feeling of being unfaithful to his wife consumed him and his stomach burned. Even though she'd gotten him to promise to remarry, he'd known that he never would love another as he had loved her. He'd found comfort in knowing that his heart was safe from ever breaking that way again.

Now Carmen was storming his barriers and threatening to break into his heart. She was caring and compassionate, treating everyone she encountered with kindness. Robyn adored her. Even Alyssa seemed fond of her. The more Trent himself was around her, the more he liked her. For the first time since Anna's death he could imagine himself falling in love.

He would never allow that to happen. Anna was his one love. His only love. Carmen's two weeks in town were up. Tomorrow he would remind her of that fact. He needed her to leave.

That decided, he wandered to the kitchen, hoping for inspiration for dinner. Although neither girl had complained, he knew they were sick of the eternal string of casseroles he'd warmed up nearly every night since Mrs. Watson left town. His stomach rebelled at the thought of choking down one more bite.

He opened and closed cabinets and the refrigerator. Nothing looked appetizing. Pizza. Maybe he could convince Alyssa to go out for pizza with him. The two of them rarely spent time alone together. Since Robyn was spending the night with Juliet, this was the perfect opportunity. Who knew, maybe pizza would get Alyssa out of the snit she was in.

She'd been ecstatic while working on the mural. He'd made a point of walking by her regularly. Each time he saw her, she was laughing and having a great time. But something had changed. She hadn't said one word on the drive home. The second he'd let them into the house, she'd raced to her room and slammed the door. She'd been in there ever since.

Having settled on his pizza idea, he sprinted up the stairs to her room. He started to knock but paused with his hand in the air. He could hear her crying.

"Alyssa?"

"Go away."

"You know I can't do that."

"Why not? You don't care how I feel."

Her words pierced his heart. "You know that's not true." Silence.

"I'm coming in." He stepped inside the room and his heart stopped. His daughter was leaning against her headboard, a pillow clutched to her chest. Her eyes and nose were red, her face wet. He sat on the foot of the bed. "Why are you crying? Has someone done something to hurt you? Are those kids still being mean?"

She shook her head.

"What? Alyssa, I want to help, but I can't if you don't let me."

She wiped her eyes on her sleeve. "There's nothing you can do. Not about this."

"Tell me. Let me try."

"She's leaving."

"Who?"

"Carmen." She hiccuped. "After the picnic, I went back to the center with Joseph. Carmen was still there. She told me she's going back to New York tomorrow." Alyssa's sobs grew louder. "She came here for her mother's funeral, but now she's going home."

Trent grabbed a tissue from the bedside table and handed it to her. "You knew she was only visiting."

She nodded, ignoring the tissue in favor of her shirt. "I just hoped she would like it here and decide to stay. Everything is better with her around. I don't feel so lonely. I wish she wouldn't go."

Trent groaned inwardly. He didn't want Carmen to stay. He needed her to leave before his emotions got out of control. "You know she has a job in New York. She has to get back to work so she can support herself."

"She's an artist. I thought they could work anywhere. Joseph says all he needs is canvas and paint. We have that here."

Trent was already sick of hearing Joseph's name. "I don't know what being an artist involves. I imagine she needs to talk to gallery owners and get them to show her work. She can't do that from here."

Alyssa sighed as if there was nothing good in her world. She finally took the tissue and began to shred it. "I guess. It's just that with Carmen around, it felt like when…"

"When what?"

"When Mom was alive. Carmen really cares about me. I know she cares about everyone, but I think she cares about me more. Like I'm special."

Trent didn't know what to say to that. He didn't want Alyssa comparing Carmen to her mother. There was no comparison. Anna had been perfect and Carmen was… Well, Carmen was…not Anna. "You are special."

Alyssa shrugged. "What did you want?"

Discussion over.

"I wanted to see if you want to get a pizza. Just you and me. What do you say?"

She was shaking her head before he even finished speaking. "No. I'm not hungry. I ate a lot at the cookout."

"How about a movie?"

"No. I want to be alone."

He fumbled for something comforting to say, but nothing came to mind. Finally, he stood. "I might go out for a while. Will you be all right here alone?"

She rolled her eyes. "I'm not a baby. Of course I'll be all right."

"I didn't mean— Never mind." He risked her wrath and kissed her damp cheek. This time she didn't pull away.

He was nearly out the door of her room when he heard her whisper, "I wish she wouldn't leave."

Trent argued with himself on the drive to the B and B. He didn't want Carmen to stay, but Alyssa needed her. Somehow she had managed to reach his daughter. As a father, he would do anything for his child, including asking Carmen to remain in Sweet Briar. But, he wondered, was he also asking for himself?

Chapter Twelve

"What are you doing here?" Carmen asked, leaning against the door. She knew she sounded rude, but there was no need to pretend she and Trent Knight were friends even if he made her heart gallop. Especially since he made her heart gallop.

He blew out a breath. "May I come in?"

She stepped back. "This is a surprise."

"I hope I didn't interrupt anything."

"No." The quaint room was not designed for entertaining. With only one chair, seating was limited. She waved him to the chair and settled on the bed. Having him sit where she slept felt too intimate.

She inhaled, trying to fill her lungs, and got a whiff of clean male with just the right hint of aftershave. He didn't speak as he looked around. Did he have any idea how he overwhelmed the room?

"You wanted to talk to me?" she prompted, when she could no longer stand the silence.

"Yes. I spoke to Alyssa. She said you're returning to New York."

"Tomorrow. So if you came to make sure I'm leaving, you wasted your time. I have my plane ticket. As you can see, my bags are packed." She gestured to the suitcase beside the dresser.

She stood, hoping he would take the hint. It hurt, knowing he couldn't wait to see the back of her.

He didn't stand.

Instead, he gestured to the bed. "Please sit down."

She hesitated, then perched on the edge of the bed. Despite the fact that their relationship was strained at best, she found herself noticing little things about him she shouldn't. Like the way the powerful muscles in his thighs moved as he shifted his legs. Or the way his faded T-shirt molded his sculpted chest and shoulders. Or the thick lashes framing his dark eyes. There were plenty of good-looking men in New York, but none of them had his rugged appeal.

"Alyssa has grown quite fond of you."

Carmen's smile came easily. "The feeling is mutual."

"She was upset tonight. She doesn't want you to leave."

"I bet you hate that. I bet you can't wait for me to be gone."

He steepled his fingers. "Truth? I'm torn. It would be less complicated if you were gone. But…"

Carmen's stupid heart skipped a beat. "But what?"

"Alyssa's been having a rough go of it."

"I know. I've tried to help."

He nodded, then his head shot up. He pierced her with his eyes. "Why?"

"Why was I trying to help?"

"Yes."

She sighed and then walked to the window. A slight breeze blew, ruffling the leaves on the trees. An owl hooted in the distance. "A couple of reasons. First, I know what it's like to be an outsider."

"You?"

"Yeah, me."

"Your family is the richest in town and one of the richest in the state. Most people in Sweet Briar either work for your father or know someone who does. He was the puppet master, controlling both the former mayor and chief of police. I can't picture you being an outsider."

"Think about it. Kids whose parents worked for my father were told to be nice to me. How about that for a sure-fire way to kill a potential friendship? Not that my father would have allowed me to be friends with them. He had his own ideas of who we should associate with. My sisters went along with him, but I couldn't. I wanted to choose my own friends.

"Charlotte actually got engaged to some guy because my father wanted her to. She'd be Mrs. Rick Tyler if he hadn't left her standing at the altar. Who picks their kid's husband like that? And who lets their father do it?" Carmen gave a laugh that was half anger, half disbelief.

"Grammar school was okay. The problem started once I got to high school. The other kids resented me, so I started hanging out with kids who didn't care who my father was. They got into a lot of trouble. There was drinking and even worse stuff. I wouldn't choose to hang out with those people now, but then?" She shrugged. "You know better than anyone how that ended."

She paced from the window to the bed and then back. Amazing how much smaller the room seemed with Chief Knight in it. "Not only was I an outsider at school, I was one at home. When I wouldn't hang out with the kids my father preferred, or dress in the clothes he selected, he decided I wasn't good enough to be his child."

She looked out the window at the growing darkness. Somehow, looking away from the chief made it easier to confide such painful secrets. That, and knowing she'd never see him again.

"Do you know why I don't use the Shields name professionally? My father told me repeatedly I wasn't worthy of it. For the longest time I believed it. I was scared that if I used it, he'd find out and get angry. So I use my middle name instead."

She stared into space, remembering those first difficult years when she'd struggled to believe in herself and her worth. She wondered whether knowing how well-received her paintings were and how much money she made from them would make her father sorry she didn't use the Shields name.

"You said there were a couple of reasons you were helping Alyssa. What was the other?"

"I kind of promised." She glanced over at the chief. He was staring at her intently. There was no anger in his stare, thank goodness. There was curiosity, though. And unexpected kindness.

"Remember when you saw me at your wife's grave?"

He nodded.

"I didn't know she'd died. When you told me, I knew I had to try to make amends. So I promised her I would do whatever I could to make things better for her family."

He raised an eyebrow. "Her family?"

"Well, her daughters. It didn't take long to realize the only thing I could do for you was leave."

When he didn't deny it, her heart sank a little. Did she really believe he could come to care about her? She forged on. "It was clear Alyssa was being ostracized. So I became her friend. And tried to help her make one in Joseph."

"And Robyn?"

"She's a darling. That girl's a matchmaker on a mission. You'd better watch out or she'll sign you up on an internet dating site."

He grimaced. "Thanks for giving me a new nightmare."

Carmen grinned. "I live to please. Anyway, it's obvious she loves you as much as you love her. But she longs for a mother's love. She told me she's going to find a mommy."

"It sounds as if you love them."

She nodded. "I didn't think it through. I meant to do something good, but it turns out I messed up."

"How?"

"You said Alyssa is upset that I'm going back to New York. I never meant for that to happen."

"I know."

"You're not going to scream at me? Tell me I should have asked you first?"

"Nah."

"Then why are you here?"

Why was he here? Good question.

"I need to ask you something."

"Okay." She tilted her head, and her hair brushed her shoulder. It was styled differently than when she'd arrived in town. Then it had been straight. Sedate. Now it was wavy, giving her a more carefree look. He liked it.

"What does your job involve?"

Her mouth dropped open. "You want to ask about my job?"

He rubbed a hand down his face. "I'm messing this up. I know you plan to leave tomorrow. Do you have to or can you stay longer?"

"You want me to stay?" Her eyes glowed with what could only be described as joy. In that moment, she was so beautiful she took his breath away. He clamped down on a desire that came from out of nowhere.

"I don't want you to stay for me." He needed to clear that up right away. For both of them. When the light faded from her eyes, he realized he'd said it wrong. But he didn't want her to believe he was falling for her.

"Oh." She brushed her hands over her smooth thighs. Although no more than five-four, she had impossibly long legs. "There are several facets to my job. I generally paint what I want and take it to a gallery that shows my work. Recently, I received a request from an individual to create a piece specifically for him."

"Why are you telling me this?"

"You asked."

Had he? "Right. I just wanted to know if you could do your work in Sweet Briar."

She shrugged. "I can paint here, but there are parts of my job that can only be done in New York. Why?"

"You've bonded with Alyssa in a way no one else has."

"I've been her. She's hurt and confused and thinks no one is on her side."

"I am, but she can't see that. Our relationship is broken. I'm hoping you can help us put it back together."

"Me? I can't fix my relationship with my own family. They won't even speak to me."

"And Alyssa won't speak to me. I don't want us to end up like you and your father."

"You won't. You actually love her."

"So much so I'm begging you to stay. Please. She needs you." He needed her.

Carmen was silent. He wondered what she was thinking. He hoped she wasn't recalling how poorly he'd treated her. How he'd told her she wasn't wanted here. The irony of him pleading with her to stay wasn't lost on him.

"If you think I can help, I suppose I can stay. After all, I did promise. I need to reschedule a couple of meetings, but that shouldn't be a problem."

"Thank you."

She stared at him, seeing clear to his soul. "This was hard for you."

"I hate asking for favors."

"It must be worse because it's me."

He couldn't deny it, but he didn't want to hurt her feelings. "I love my daughter."

"Me, too."

"Do we have a deal?"

Carmen thrust out her hand and he took it into his. Her hand was so soft, so tiny, yet the contact packed a wallop. It was like being electrocuted.

He was in trouble.

Chapter Thirteen

"Carmen, you're here!" Surprise and pleasure filled Alyssa's voice.

Carmen marked her place in the book and rose from the blanket. She smiled at Alyssa as the teen raced across the grass, Robyn not far behind. Their father followed at a distance. The day was bright and sunny, but surprisingly few people had chosen to spend time at the park.

"I'm glad to see you, too," Carmen replied, more than a little pleased at the girls' enthusiasm. Their joy confirmed she'd made the right decision when she'd agreed to stay.

"Daddy said you were staying in town and that I'd see you at the youth center tomorrow. This is way better. I'm glad you're still here. I was going to miss you."

"I would have missed you, too." Carmen hugged Alyssa, her smile broadening when the teen hugged her back.

"Hey, what about me?" Robyn elbowed her way past her sister to join the embrace.

"I would have missed you, too," Carmen said, wrapping her free arm around the younger girl and giving her a little squeeze. She closed her eyes and enjoyed the wonderful moment. She liked all the children in town, but these two had a special place in her heart.

"How long can you stay?" Alyssa asked, looking Carmen directly in the eye. Like father like daughter.

"I'm not sure." She had rescheduled her meetings and arranged to handle everything else by phone until her next gallery showing. Of course, if a problem arose, she'd have to fly back. But if all went according to plan, she would be around to help get Alyssa through this difficult time, and help Trent get the father-daughter relationship back on track.

She glanced at Trent. There was an unreadable expression on his face and he wore sunglasses, so she couldn't see his eyes. Not that it mattered. His eyes never gave anything away.

He was holding the strings to a trio of kites that bobbed behind him, lifted by the gentle breeze.

"How about forever?" Robyn suggested. She grabbed Carmen's hand and swung it back and forth.

"She can't stay forever. She has to show her work in galleries sometimes," Alyssa said authoritatively. She then smiled shyly at Carmen. "But maybe you can stay for the rest of the summer."

"I'd like to," Carmen said, daring to glance at Trent. Nothing. He was a master of the poker face.

"Yay!" Robyn exclaimed, jumping up and down, nearly pulling Carmen's arm out of its socket.

"Hold on. I'd like to, but I have a showing in three weeks. I have to go back then."

"Will you have to stay after the show?" Alyssa asked, a cautious, yet hopeful expression on her face.

"For a few days. Maybe a week. It depends on what's going on."

Alyssa smiled again. "Okay. At least you'll be here for the girls versus boys basketball tournament next Saturday. It's a lot of fun. Since I'm in high school now, I'll get to play."

"That's great. I'll cheer you on."

"You don't have to just cheer. You can play. All the volunteers do."

"Really?"

"Yeah. The guys won last year and they did a whole lot of bragging."

Carmen turned to Trent. "I can't imagine you bragging."

"Daddy didn't play." Like Trent, Alyssa had perfected the poker face, but her voice gave away disappointment.

"He never plays," Robyn added matter-of-factly.

"I'm going to play this year."

That brought him three surprised looks. Carmen couldn't picture him being willing to shed his authoritative persona and take on a role of team player. She could, however, picture his muscular legs in shorts and his broad chest in a sweaty T-shirt.

"You are?" Alyssa asked, smiling brightly.

"Yes." He removed his sunglasses and tucked them into the collar of his shirt.

Alyssa didn't reply, but the expression on her face was beyond thrilled.

Robyn stooped down and picked up a smooth rock. She examined it from every side, then drew back her arm and threw it as far as she could. "I'm glad you're here," she told Carmen. "We always come to the park to fly kites after Sunday school."

"It's such a nice day I thought I'd spend some time

outside enjoying it. I brought a book and bread to feed the ducks."

"Is that your picnic basket?"

Carmen laughed as Robyn edged around the blanket. "Yes."

"It sure is big." Robyn lifted the lid and peeked inside.

"Robyn," Trent warned, then flashed Carmen a rueful grin that warmed her all the way to her toes. "Sorry."

"It's okay. It's not like she can hurt anything. Besides, I'm curious to know what's in there, too."

"You don't know what you have?" Alyssa asked, raising an eyebrow.

"Nope. Last night I told Joni I was going to stay in town longer. She showed up at the B and B a little while ago with food and suggested I come here. She said it was a thank-you for the mural, but I think she wants to remind me that I won't get food as good as Brandon's in New York." And maybe her friend was doing a little bit of matchmaking. But Carmen could have told Joni it was hopeless.

"Mr. Danielson is a great cook. He cooks better than Mrs. Watson." Alyssa twisted her hair around a finger, then continued, "I used to think it was weird for a man to be a cook, but not anymore."

Alyssa turned her attention to Robyn, who had gone from just peeking into the basket to removing covered containers.

Carmen smiled and inclined her head. "Maybe you should help her."

Alyssa giggled and hurried to join her sister.

"Sorry," Trent said.

"For what?"

"For crashing your picnic. I imagine you came here for some peace and quiet. Instead, you've got the entire Knight family hanging around. We should go."

"No, stay." She reached out and grabbed his arm. Insane sparks shot from her hand to her stomach, which immediately began to turn cartwheels.

He looked at her hand, and before she could pull back, he covered it with his own. His large palm was calloused, yet his touch was gentle. His eyes probed hers and in their depths she saw a need to touch and be touched in return. "Thank you for telling the girls you would stay awhile. It means a lot to both of them. To all of us."

"You're welcome."

He stared at her for a moment. Then, as if realizing he was still holding her hand, he released it and stepped back, creating distance between them. She immediately felt the loss of his warmth.

"Are you sure we aren't intruding?"

When he touched her, she wasn't sure about anything, including her name. "Positive."

"All right." A smile started at the edge of his mouth, slowly turning into a broad grin. His eyes began to twinkle. "But I have to warn you that any minute someone is going to be begging for food."

Carmen smiled. "That's okay," she replied, looking over her shoulder at his girls. "I don't mind sharing."

"I meant me," he said, and they both laughed. "I love Brandon's cooking, too."

"Then by all means, let's see what he made. I'd love to share my lunch with the entire Knight family."

Trent secured the kites and he and Carmen joined the girls, who had removed all the containers from the basket.

"Brownies!" Robyn exclaimed, as she pulled the lid off a large purple tub. "I love brownies."

"Me, too," Alyssa added.

"Well, then, what do you say we get this picnic started?" Carmen said.

Ten minutes later they were sitting in a circle, eating chicken, pasta salad, strawberries and brownies. Joni had packed more food than Carmen would ever have been able to eat, confirming her suspicion that her friend had known Trent would appear with his daughters. If he thought it odd she had food for four, he kept it to himself.

After the girls finished eating, they grabbed the bread and walked to the water's edge to feed the ducks.

"I'll watch her, Dad," Alyssa called over her shoulder.

"They're very close," Carmen said, as she watched the girls walk away.

"Yes. As angry as Alyssa can get with me, she's always kind and loving to Robyn. I can count on one hand the times she's lost patience with her over the years."

"Alyssa is a good girl. You must be proud."

"Thanks." His lips turned down slightly. "I just wish she would talk to me like she used to. She used to say I was her best friend. Now half the time she treats me like I'm her worst enemy."

"It's hard for a teenage girl to confide in her dad."

"Maybe. I wouldn't mind so much if she had a mother to talk to. But she doesn't. I'm all she has."

"Thanks to me."

He gripped her chin between his thumb and forefinger, lifting it until their eyes met. "I thought we settled that. The accident wasn't your fault."

"I guess it's going to take me a while to believe you really don't blame me for taking your wife away."

"Given the way I treated you, that's understandable." He pulled up a blade of grass and twisted it between two long fingers. His nails were neat and clean. They weren't the manicured nails of a pampered male, but those of a man's man, one who wasn't overly fussy about his appearance.

"You know, when I asked you to stay, I didn't give much thought to the disruption we're causing to your life."

"It's not a problem."

"You have a show. I imagine that will involve doing more than turning up and looking beautiful."

Her heart thumped. Did he think she was beautiful? In her dreams. He was still in love with his perfect wife. "It does. But I can handle a lot from here. What I can't do, the gallery owner will. I'll fly up a couple of days ahead of time to deal with any last-minute details."

"I really appreciate it."

"I don't mind. I'm enjoying my stay in Sweet Briar. I'd forgotten how beautiful it was. How relaxing." She closed her eyes and lifted her face to the sky. The sun warmed her skin even as a slight breeze cooled it.

"Not missing New York?"

She thought for a moment and then opened her eyes to meet his gaze. She'd never seen his eyes look so kind. "Not really. I like parts of New York, but it's never truly become my home. I miss my friend Damon, of course, but he and I talk every night."

Trent's lips compressed in what looked like annoyance, but maybe she was misreading him. He had no reason to be irritated with Damon. They'd never met. If they ever did, Trent would love the man. Everyone did.

"So tell me, how did you become the artist to watch this century?"

Carmen dropped her face into her hands. "Please tell me you didn't read that ridiculous article."

"I confess I Googled you. I think I've read just about every word written about you. According to the critics, your work is profound yet accessible. Easily understood by the masses." He lifted his nose and spoke in what she supposed was his upper-class voice.

She giggled. She never would have believed Trent would joke with her.

"So how did you get there from here?"

"You mean from being the wild child of Sweet Briar to an artist?"

"Yeah."

He waited while Carmen took a sip of her water. He had a feeling she was stalling.

"After my father put me out, I didn't know what to do or where to go. I had very little money and didn't want to waste it on a bus ticket. So I just started walking down the highway. Three girls on their way to New York hoping to get modeling jobs stopped and offered me a ride. I took it. They had rented an apartment for the summer and let me stay with them."

She glanced at him, a desolate look on her face that just about broke his heart. "Unlike me, they weren't castoffs, so when their plans didn't pan out, they went back home to start college."

She sighed. "I called my father to see if I could come back, but he said no and hung up."

Her eyes were dry, but overflowing with misery. "You're a father. I know Alyssa's been giving you a hard time. She's been really angry at you. Is there anything she could do that would make you stop loving her?"

"Nothing. No matter what she does, she's my child. That will never change."

Carmen nodded. "I knew you would say that. I could tell. My father doesn't feel the same way. Not that what I did is the same as being disrespectful. It was many times worse. I know being sorry doesn't change anything, but I am."

Trent squeezed her hand. It was warm and soft. Delicate. "I know that. You don't have to tell me that again."

"That's what I don't understand. You've forgiven me and I'm grateful. Why won't my father?"

"I don't know. As a parent, it doesn't make sense." Trent would never turn his back on his children.

Carmen hugged her shins, placing her head on her knees. "Anyway, my roommates went back home. They knew I was on my own, so they left me some of their clothes. The rent was paid for the next couple of weeks, but there wasn't a lot of food. I know it was wrong, but I shoplifted. And before you call me a criminal, I paid the stores back double when I got a job."

"I wasn't going to call you a criminal." It hurt that she assumed he couldn't sympathize with her situation. Worse was knowing that, once, she would have been right. He'd become hard and unfeeling after Anna died. Only recently, since he'd begun to really know Carmen, had he begun to change. The world wasn't as black-and-white as he'd seen it for seven years.

She straightened and crossed her ankles, the movement drawing attention to her shapely legs. She even had pretty feet. Although she didn't wear polish on her fingernails, her toenails were painted a bright pink.

"I couldn't find a job, so I lost my apartment. That was a scary time."

She didn't say anything for a long moment. Fear gripped him and his stomach clenched. He knew what could happen to a young girl with no one to look out for her. "So what did you do?"

"I shoved everything I could into a backpack. The first night was the scariest. I didn't have a plan. Unless you've been there, you have no idea how terrifying it is to have no place to call home. I lived in fear, knowing someone could grab me off the street and no one would ever know. Or care."

His heart pounded at the thought of her being kidnapped and hurt. Or worse.

"I finally found a diner that was open twenty-four hours. I had some change, so I bought a cup of coffee and nursed it all night."

He closed his eyes, feeling a wave of pain. She'd been only a few years older than Alyssa when she had to fend for herself. "What about shelters?"

"They fill up really fast. And they aren't always safe, either. Especially for girls."

Horrifying possibilities flooded his mind. Had she been hurt? Assaulted? The thought was heartbreaking.

"One day I stumbled upon the library. I could sit there for hours and no one would bother me. They have little rooms for studying. I would grab a stack of books and hide in there and sleep. I'd stay there until closing. Then it was back to the streets."

"I'm so sorry."

"Of all the people in the world, you are one who never has to apologize to me for anything."

"Even so, I'm sorry for everything you endured." He couldn't bear to hear any more. "So how did you go from being homeless to being a much sought-after artist?"

"Luck. And a wonderful friend. I told you I spent a lot of time at the library."

He nodded.

"One day this guy came up to me. I'd noticed him a couple of times, which was pretty strange, given the number of people in that city. But then I figured he was a creature of habit. You know, like maybe his office was nearby and he liked to go to the library."

Trent's blood ran cold at the mention of the man. Young girls were often targeted by older men. Especially when they had no one to protect them. His hand fisted.

"Anyway, I was sitting at a table when he sat down across from me. I was a little scared, because there were plenty of empty tables. He must have seen my fear, because he told me he wasn't going to hurt me. He was going to help me."

Trent frowned. "I hope you got away from him. Offering help is one of the most common ways pimps prey on vulnerable girls."

"That's what I thought, too. I told him that I didn't need help, but he didn't listen. He gave me his business card and twenty dollars so I could get some food. And then he left."

"I hope you went straight to the police."

"No. I had no intention of calling him, but I took the money. I was hungry. The next day I sat in a different place in the library. He found me and gave me another card and twenty dollars again. This went on for a couple of weeks.

"Finally, I asked him why he kept giving me money. He showed me a picture of a little girl about Robyn's age. The girl was his daughter. When she was little, he was trying to build his company, so he didn't spend much time with her. She died in a swimming accident. He'd made millions, but it was too late. He knew I was in trouble. He hadn't been there for her, but he wanted to help me."

"And you believed him?"

"Of course not. I used the library computer and looked him up on the internet. Everything he said was true. So the next time I saw him I asked him for a job at his company."

"Good move."

"I still didn't trust him, but I was so tired and miserable. He told me to meet him at his office at nine o'clock the next day. I did and I became a secretary slash administrative assistant slash mailroom clerk."

She smiled. "I didn't have a clue how to do my job, but

that didn't matter. They trained me. Apparently, I wasn't the first girl Damon had rescued."

"So this guy was legit?"

"Yes. He really did only want to help me."

Trent's shoulders relaxed and he sighed in relief. "You took a big risk."

Carmen shrugged. "I was alone. I had no job. No family. No nothing. I didn't see my life ever improving. Damon knew this sweet old lady who ran a rooming house. He paid her in advance for six months. It was such a relief to have a place to live.

"Damon and I talked every day. I told him about my dream to become an artist. He paid for me to go to school and helped me get my first job at an art gallery."

"He sounds like a good guy."

She smiled. "The best."

"I'm glad he was there for you."

"Me, too. And now I can pass it on. I can be there for Alyssa."

Trent smiled back. Maybe she could be there for him, too. He quickly shoved the thought away, reminding himself that he didn't want her in his life.

Chapter Fourteen

"I can't believe I let you talk me into this," Carmen said, looking around the gym. It was packed to the rafters with teens and adults alike. Little kids raced around and chased each other up and down the bleachers. The scent of freshly popped popcorn wafted over from the concession stand. Carmen would much rather be among the spectators than players, but it was too late now.

She put her foot on the bench and worked a knot out of her shoelace.

Joni smiled. "It's for a good cause. Besides, you'll have fun."

Carmen retied her shoe and stood. "Tell me again why running up and down the floor is fun."

"It's basketball."

"And?" Carmen stretched the word over three syllables. "Basketball doesn't equal fun to me. And I certainly can't imagine why it would be entertaining for all these people to watch."

"Trust me, it just is. We started the basketball tournament two years ago. It's one of our biggest and most popular fund-raisers. You'll have a great time."

"I doubt it. I'll probably trip and fall on my face in the middle of the field."

"Court."

"What?"

"You said field. Basketball is played on a court."

"You just proved my point."

"What point?" Joni asked, gathering her hair in one hand and quickly wrapping a bright orange ponytail holder around it with the other.

Carmen wondered if she should do the same. She'd spent the morning styling her hair until it fell in waves around her shoulders. She'd even spritzed on perfume, something she rarely did. Although she barely admitted it to herself, she wanted to look attractive for Trent. She didn't think wild hair and sweat stains were her best look. "People who don't know the difference between a field and a court have no business playing sports."

Joni laughed. "Lighten up. It's just good fun."

"Sure it is. That's why they're practicing so hard." Carmen pointed to the guys' team. They were in two lines, passing the ball back and forth, taking turns shooting baskets. They were highly coordinated and focused. From where Carmen stood, they were taking the tournament seriously.

"That's nothing," Joni said, dismissing Carmen's worry with a wave of her hand. "We'll warm up, too."

"They haven't missed yet. And they're wearing uniforms with numbers and names on the back. They even have matching shoestrings."

"That's to build team spirit. If you want, I have an

extra scrunchie. It's not orange, but then you're not wearing orange."

No. Unlike the guys, who were dressed in blue and white, the women wore whatever color suited them best. For Carmen, that was a green T-shirt and white shorts.

"So, you girls ready to lose again?" Lex asked, as he and Trent joined them.

"Don't go engraving your name on the trophy just yet," Joni said. "We're going to wipe the floor with you this year."

"Not to brag," Lex said, poking out his chest, "but we did win all but one game last year."

"Brag all you want. After today, we'll have that privilege," Joni said, punching the mayor in the arm.

Trent laughed and looked at Carmen. "Get out while you can."

Carmen smiled back, trying not to notice how good he looked in his sleeveless white jersey that showed off an incredible chest and perfectly sculpted biceps and shoulders. If she had her way, he'd never wear sleeves again. "You're awfully cocky for someone who's never seen me play basketball."

"Oooh. Tall talk from one so small. Care to wager on the outcome of the tournament?"

Carmen leaned in close enough to get a whiff of his masculine scent and promptly went weak in the knees. "Betting? Isn't gambling illegal in Sweet Briar? That sounds like entrapment to me, Chief."

"I won't tell if you won't. Besides, I'm not talking about money." He wiggled his eyebrows.

"Then what?" She couldn't believe it. He was flirting with her and she was flirting right back. The sensible part of her told her to stop but was quickly overruled by the woman who found Trent too sexy to resist.

He leaned down and whispered in her ear, his warm breath stirring her hair and sending shivers down her spine. "Dinner. When my team wins, you'll take me to dinner."

"And when my team wins?"

"You'll wake up and realize it was only a dream."

"Ha-ha."

"Okay. I'll take *you* to dinner."

She held out her hand. "Deal."

He stared at her hand and then at her mouth for one long moment. He gave her a sexy half smile and took her hand in his. It was more of a caress than a handshake. "Deal."

Carmen watched the chief walk away, a definite swagger in his step.

"Well, well, it appears things are moving right along with you and Trent. I guess my little picnic worked."

Carmen giggled like a teenager. "Maybe."

"Too bad you can't play as good a game as you talk."

"I know."

"Lucky for you, I have a secret weapon this year."

"What? You hired one of the Carter boys to tie all the guys' shoestrings together so they'll fall?"

Joni laughed and shook her head. "What is it with you and shoestrings? Never mind. Our secret weapon just arrived."

Joni waved at six very tall women dressed in bright red warm-ups who were stepping down the stairs with graceful ease. Not thin enough to be models, they were clearly in great shape. Joni greeted them and then turned to Carmen. "Let me introduce you to the Central Carolina University women's basketball team, reigning NCAA Division II champions."

Carmen gasped and then burst out laughing. "Are you serious? How do you plan on getting away with this? I thought all of the participants had to be volunteers or kids who use the center."

"We each volunteered at least one day during the past year," one of the players said, as she stretched from side to side.

"But none of them played basketball," Joni added. "They worked the front desk or served snacks."

"You are so sneaky," Carmen said, clapping her hands with glee. "I wish I'd thought of it. More important, I'm glad I won't have to play."

"Not so fast there, benchwarmer," Joni said, grabbing her arm before she could make her escape. "You're still playing."

"But I don't know how. I'll make us lose. Besides, you don't need me." And call her vain, but Carmen didn't want to get all sweaty and smelly in front of Trent. She had a feeling perspiration wouldn't look as good on her as it would on him.

"You'll be fine. You'll only be playing in the first game. And only the first quarter."

"Twenty-five minutes? I'll have a heart attack and die. Or at least faint and fall to the floor in a heap."

The others laughed.

"Who told you a quarter was twenty-five minutes?" Joni asked.

"I just guessed. You know, twenty-five cents is a quarter."

"And ten cents is a dime, but that has nothing to do with basketball. We're playing six-minute quarters with an eight-minute halftime so our cheerleaders can shake their things. We have six games to play. Most of the kids play in about three or four games each, more if they want. Our best team will play in the championship round."

"Six minutes and I'm done?"

Joni rolled her eyes. "Is that all you heard?"

"I just don't want to make us lose. Or get all mussed." Carmen glanced to where Trent stood, looking sexy and powerful enough to make her mouth water. He must have felt her eyes on him, because he looked up and winked. Her cheeks warmed as she returned her focus to her team.

"Don't worry," one of the college girls added. "All you have to do is run up and down the court. As long as you don't trip and fall on your face, you'll be fine."

Ten minutes later, Carmen dropped into the first empty chair and grabbed a water bottle.

"See, it wasn't that bad," Joni said, taking the seat beside her.

"Compared to what?" Carmen twisted open the cap and took two less-than-dainty swallows. She would never be the same.

Joni laughed. "You need to be more active."

"I'm plenty active. Remember, I did borrow your bike."

"Coasting to the park doesn't count."

"Okay, so I'm a couch potato. Someone has to make the rest of the world feel better about itself by comparison."

"And you're doing a wonderful job."

"Not nearly as wonderful as they are. Those girls are fabulous." She waved the nearly empty water bottle toward the floor, where two of the college girls were teamed with Alyssa and two other teens. Alyssa made a basket and Carmen jumped to her feet, cheering loudly, her aching body momentarily forgotten.

"Yeah. And look at the expressions on Lex's and Trent's faces. They can't believe they're only leading by two."

"We'd be winning if I hadn't tripped and lost the ball." Trent had been guarding her. He'd gotten close enough for her to feel the heat radiating from his chest. She'd gotten flustered and forgotten how to walk.

"At least you didn't fall."

"Yeah. There is that."

"Besides, we don't have to win all of the games. Only the last one, which will be their best players against ours."

"I'm assuming I'm not on that team."

Joni grinned. "No. You just missed the cut."

"I must be living right."

They laughed and then turned their attention back to the game. Trent and Lex were teamed with three boys Carmen had seen around the center. She told herself to follow the action, but her eyes kept straying to Trent.

Although he was nearing forty, his body was like that of a man in his late twenties. He was ripped. Not only did he have muscles, he had stamina. He raced up and down the court with ease, frequently a step or two ahead of the young guys.

He stole the ball from a blonde girl who appeared more interested in a boy sitting on the bench than in playing the game, then dribbled down the court. Trent dunked the ball, hanging on the rim for several seconds, clearly showing off. His eyes met Carmen's and her breath caught in her throat. A kid ran past them, breaking their eye contact, and she exhaled.

What was Trent doing to her?

"From here it looks like serious flirtation."

Carmen spun around and looked into Joni's smiling face.

"Don't worry. Your secret is safe."

"What secret?" And just how spooky was it that Joni knew exactly what she was thinking?

"That the lawman is stealing your heart," Joni quipped, as she walked away.

Carmen forced herself to focus on the action on the court and not the thoughts bouncing around in her head like a basketball. Fortunately, there was only a minute left. The girls ran down the floor, passing the ball back and forth until only a few seconds remained. A college girl took a shot that went in as the buzzer went off. The girls had won the game.

A cheer went up and the players gathered at the benches as the cheerleaders rushed to center court. Trent left his team, coming to stand in front of Carmen.

"I guess this means you're taking me to dinner," she said, grinning.

"Not so fast. Your team hasn't won the trophy yet, although you seem to have some ringers on your side."

"They're volunteers."

"Who just happen to play college basketball?"

Carmen's grin broadened. "Yeah, that, too."

Trent laughed. "Okay, but don't be too disappointed when we win. We have quite a few good young players."

"It's going to take more than that. We've got great players," she called, as he rejoined his team. As she watched him, Joni's words came back to her.

Her friend had been wrong. Trent wasn't stealing her heart. He'd already stolen it.

Her smile faded as she realized that was the worst thing that could happen. Because even if he no longer hated her, she knew she'd never have *his* heart. His heart would always belong to Anna.

Chapter Fifteen

"Three, two, one!" The crowd cheered as the buzzer went off. The final game was over and the women had won. No surprise there, given that the players in the deciding game were college athletes. Trent grinned despite himself. That trick had to have taken a great deal of planning.

"Well, that's it. Good game." Trent met the eyes of each of his players as he patted them on the shoulder. They'd surprised and impressed him. Although most could use a good haircut, several were in need of belts and many in need of more direction than they received at home, they were good young men. He never would have believed that a month ago. Of course, a month ago he hadn't spent time getting to know them.

"Thanks, Chief."

"Line up for the handshakes. And be sure to smile when you congratulate the other team."

"Joni is never going to let me live this down," Lex grumbled, coming up beside Trent.

Trent laughed but didn't disagree. Joni was going to tease them mercilessly. Lex might be dreading the next moments, but Trent was looking forward to them. Despite the razzing that was sure to come, he was anticipating paying his debt to Carmen.

After the players returned to their benches, someone dragged a microphone to the middle of the court. A young man Trent didn't recognize carried out the two-foot-tall trophy.

"Let the bragging begin!" Joni pronounced, as two college girls held the trophy aloft. The rest of the women hooted and cheered. Carmen flashed Trent a saucy grin that made his pulse race.

Joni ribbed the men good-naturedly a few more times before getting serious. "Thank you all for coming. We could do nothing without your support. Each year we award a trophy to the first-place team. This year, the women have won." The crowd roared and clapped loudly.

"Will the players please come forward to pose with the championship trophy?" Joni handed the microphone to the kid who'd brought out the trophy, then joined her teammates, who were laughing and jockeying for place, finally organizing themselves around the trophy. Phil Henderson took photos for the *Sweet Briar Herald*, then stepped away.

A movement at the entrance to the gym drew Trent's eye. Carmen's sisters entered, dressed in suits much too formal for the occasion. "What are they doing here?"

"Who?" Lex asked.

Trent inclined his head toward Carmen's sisters, who had stopped just inside the door. Charmaine looked self-conscious, but Charlotte sniffed and frowned down her nose as though she was too good for the casually dressed people surrounding her.

Lex huffed out a breath. He didn't seem any more pleased by their presence than Trent. "Charlotte called me this morning. The family wants to make a donation to the center in memory of their mother. I figured one of them would drop off a check at city hall. They didn't mention wanting to do it in public today."

Of course not. Why risk being turned down? This way they could appear benevolent and let Carmen know she was not part of the family in one fell swoop.

"It looks like I need to do the mayor thing," Lex said, over the screeching sound of microphone feedback. "Keep the team together so we can take our pictures, okay?"

Trent nodded, when he really wanted to find Carmen and be by her side in case seeing her sisters disturbed her.

Lex whispered something to Joni. Eyes narrowed, she handed over the microphone.

"Before we all leave, we have a presentation from representatives of the Shields family," Lex said. "As you know, Rachel Shields donated the trophy case and the trophies for the past two years. Her daughters Charlotte and Charmaine are here to make a donation in her honor."

Trent scanned the gym and finally found Carmen. He knew the exact moment she saw her sisters. The laughter died on her lips and she went very still, clearly hurt by their continued rejection. The brilliant light he'd gotten used to seeing shining in her eyes faded to a dull brown. It took all his self-control to stay with his team and not confront Charlotte and Charmaine. He wanted to force them to see the pain they were causing their sister. It was unbelievable they would snub her in front of all these people and not give it a second thought.

"Thank you, Mayor," Charlotte said, grabbing the microphone. "Our mother believed in the mission of this youth center. She wanted the youth of this town to have a place to go to keep out of trouble. She knew that kids in trouble can ruin the lives of innocent people."

Carmen gasped, and even from a distance Trent saw her face pale. He clenched his fist and bit his tongue against the desire to voice his growing anger. There was no way Charlotte didn't know her words hurt and embarrassed Carmen. From the way she glanced at Carmen and then lifted her chin, he knew her cruel words were deliberately chosen.

"As you may know," Charlotte continued, in an annoyingly self-important tone, "our mother recently passed. Charmaine and I, along with our father, are donating five thousand dollars to the youth center in her memory. Our father is still in mourning, so Charmaine and I are representing our family."

Scattered applause greeted the announcement, certainly not as raucous as Trent would have thought, given the size of the donation. Apparently, he was not the only one unimpressed by Charlotte's performance. In her short time in Sweet Briar, Carmen had made quite a few friends. None of them liked seeing her being slighted.

Smiling graciously, Joni accepted the check on behalf of the youth center. Phil took a few shots of Joni and Lex posing with Carmen's sisters, then called for all players to come forward for a picture. Carmen edged away from the group assembled around the trophy and headed for the exit. Lex called Trent to join the picture, but he shook his head. He needed to get to Carmen.

Trent acknowledged pats on the back but didn't let anyone slow his progress. He lost track of Carmen for a minute but saw her in the parking lot. She was walking so fast she nearly bumped into a car.

"Carmen," he called. She slowed but didn't stop. He picked up his pace and easily caught up with her. He gently touched her tear-streaked face, then wrapped his arm around her shoulders, pulling her against his chest. She resisted for a brief moment, then relaxed, taking refuge in the comfort he offered. "I'm sorry. You didn't deserve that."

"I get it. I didn't at first, but now I do."

"You get what?"

Still in the circle of his embrace, she leaned back to meet his gaze. The heartbreak he saw in her eyes was nearly his undoing. "I'm not part of their family. I understood in my mind, but my heart hadn't accepted it. I kept hoping if I found the right words to apologize, they would forgive me and welcome me back into the fold. Do you know what I mean?"

He didn't trust his voice, so he nodded.

"Well, no more. I'm done with that. I'm done with them. I'm through begging. And I'm through crying." Tears dripped from her chin and she angrily brushed them away.

"You're right. You deserve better. If they don't see it, then it's their loss."

She sniffed, and despite her brave words, more tears slipped from her eyes. "Do you mind if we don't go out tonight? I don't feel up to it."

"We don't have to go out, but I don't think it's a good idea for you to be alone. How about dinner at home with me and the girls? I can throw some steaks on the grill."

She was shaking her head before he got the invitation out. "I wouldn't be very good company. I'm not at my best."

"You don't have to be."

Her chest rose and fell as she sighed. "Okay. I guess it's better than being alone."

"How much better? Are we talking better than a poke

in the eye with a sharp stick, but maybe not better than a poke with a dull stick?"

She laughed, as he intended, then shook her head. "That came out wrong."

"That's good to know."

She grinned at his dry tone. "Let me try that again. I happily accept the invitation to dine with you and your lovely daughters. Better?"

"Much better."

"There is one thing, though."

He raised an eyebrow. "And that would be…"

She stood on her tiptoes and whispered into his ear. "I don't eat beef."

He shook his head. "Of course you don't."

Carmen stood on Trent's front porch and inhaled the sweet scent of blooming roses from a nearby bush. He'd wanted her to come home with him right after the last pictures were taken, but she'd insisted on returning to the B and B so she could shower. Her comfortable shorts and T-shirt had been fine for the tournament, but she wanted something a bit dressier for dinner. Now she wore a red sundress that stopped just above her knees, paired with red-and-cream high-heeled sandals. She'd restyled her hair and put on small gold hoop earrings and a matching bracelet.

Trent's home was in the older section of town. The houses were painted in soft pastels and the lots were spacious and well kept. Trent's lawn was neatly mowed, with a large leafy tree in the center. A rope swing hung from a high branch, swaying gently in the breeze. Three boys sped by on bikes. A woman jogging with her golden retriever sang loudly and slightly off-key to the song playing through her earbuds. Two women chatted over their hedges while their children skipped rope beside them, counting by two as they jumped. Birds chirped in the trees and in the distance a dog barked. This was Sweet Briar at its best. Neighbors and friends enjoying a summer evening together.

The sound of girlish laughter wafted through Trent's open windows, stirring Carmen from her reverie.

She'd stopped by the bakery and picked up a chocolate cake for dessert. The box dangled by its strings in her right hand, so she rang the doorbell with her left.

She heard running feet seconds before the door swung open. Robyn squealed with delight, grabbed Carmen's hand and pulled her into the house.

"She's here. She's here." Robyn jumped up and down.

"So I see." Trent's deep voice was warm and welcoming.

Carmen looked up, their eyes met and her knees turned to Jell-O. His dark hair was damp from his shower. He'd changed into a lightweight gray polo that caressed his broad shoulders and emphasized the gray specks in his black eyes. A pair of faded denims hung perfectly on his trim waist and hugged his muscular thighs. How had she forgotten how gorgeous he was?

"I'm glad you came," he said. She saw a flare of desire in his eyes as he took in her appearance.

"Thanks for inviting me," she replied, dismayed when her voice came out a husky whisper. Her skin tingled as if he'd physically touched her.

"You didn't have to bring anything."

She shrugged and offered him the box. "It's just dessert. I stopped by Polly Wants A Cookie on the way here."

"Alyssa's on the phone," Robyn announced, tugging Carmen's hand. "Do you want to see my room? It's clean."

"Maybe later," Trent said. "Right now we're going out back."

"Okay," Robyn replied good-naturedly, leading Carmen through the house and to the patio. She pulled out a chair at the round glass table. "You can sit next to me."

"Thank you." Carmen smiled as she sat in the comfortable wicker chair. The blue, green and yellow stripes on the cushions matched the dishes and napkins. Somehow she hadn't pictured Trent as the type who coordinated colors. A niggling feeling started to grow, but she quashed it.

"I set the table," Robyn announced, her face alight with a proud smile.

"You did a lovely job. I've never seen a table look this pretty."

"I took everything from the mommy box."

"Mommy box?" Carmen managed to sound calm, but her unease grew.

"It's where we keep things Mommy liked. We can use them on special occasions like now."

"Oh."

"I made lemonade, too. I'll get it." She jumped from the table and hurried to the sliding doors.

"I'd better help her," Trent said, following his young daughter, totally unaware of the turmoil now brewing inside Carmen.

Get over it, she admonished herself. So he kept some of his wife's things. Some people might consider that sweet. Carmen exhaled and looked around. The backyard was a lovely expanse of dark green grass trimmed with red flowers. A white two-car garage stood at the end of the driveway. The yard was soothing and the beautiful setting helped her relax.

"Here we are," Trent announced. He was carrying a tray containing three tumblers and a glass pitcher. Lemon slices and ice cubes floated in the pale yellow liquid. Robyn trailed behind him, clenching a glass in both hands. Lemonade sloshed with every step, yet somehow none spilled over the rim.

"I have yours," Robyn said, gently setting the drink in front of Carmen.

Carmen took a sip and the bitterness of raw lemon had her swallowing a gasp. She looked into Robyn's eager face and managed a smile. "This is the best lemonade I've ever had. You're a great cook."

Robyn beamed.

"Would you please let your sister know Carmen is here?"

"Okay, Daddy." Robyn skipped across the patio and with one last wave disappeared into the house.

Carmen waited until she no longer heard the pounding of little feet before she spoke. "Quick. Get the sugar."

Trent laughed and grabbed the pitcher. "We have to do this fast. Bring your glass."

Giggling, she hurried inside, where Trent doctored the lemonade in the pitcher before sweetening hers. She took another sip and smiled. "Much better."

Still grinning, they hurried back outside. Trent poured himself a glass, then sat down, leaning back in the chair, his long legs stretched in front of him. "Thanks for being a good sport."

"No problem. Although you could have warned me."

"And missed the expression on your face? No way."

They chatted a bit about their first times cooking, laughing as they recalled meals that were as disastrous as Robyn's lemonade. Carmen was finishing off her glass when Robyn returned with Alyssa. Like Trent and Carmen, Alyssa had showered and changed. She now wore a pair of denim cutoffs and a plain gray T-shirt. Unlike other girls her age, Alyssa showed no interest in fancy clothes or makeup.

"I should get dinner started," Trent said, ambling across the patio to what was easily the largest grill Carmen had ever seen. He lifted the lid and smoke filled the air.

"Thank heaven. When I saw that monstrosity, I thought it might be a gas grill."

"No way. I use charcoal. Nothing beats that real smoky flavor."

"I agree."

"And for the record, Lulu is not a monstrosity."

"Lulu? You named your grill?" Carmen shrieked, before dissolving into giggles.

"Of course."

He managed to look so affronted Carmen only laughed harder. Tears streamed down her face.

"Daddy names everything," Robyn piped up.

"Everything?" Carmen asked.

"Yep. He named his car."

"Lots of people do that," Trent pointed out.

"Lots of men," Carmen countered.

"How many people name their bikes? Or their kites? Or their lawn mower?" Alyssa asked, chuckling.

"Hey, Herbie works hard."

"Herbie? Oh my goodness," Carmen said, bursting into laughter again. "Who would have thought it?"

He frowned, but his eyes danced. "I'm glad I could amuse you."

"You have no idea how much. Why do you name them?"

"Simple. Everything deserves a name."

"Okay. That's as good a reason as any." She refilled her glass. "Is there anything I can do to help?"

"Not a thing. You just sit there and keep the chef company. I've got it all handled."

A half hour later, he grabbed a garden salad from the fridge, topped off everyone's drinks and set a platter of perfectly grilled food on the table. In deference to Carmen he had foregone steak, instead grilling chicken breasts, whole catfish and shrimp. Corn on the cob completed the meal.

The conversation was light and the evening was enjoyable. Carmen couldn't remember when she'd had a nicer time.

"How old were you when you started dating?" Alyssa asked, when they were finished with the main course.

"You don't have to answer that," Trent said, fixing his older daughter with a hard stare. "We've already discussed it and decided that Alyssa is too young to date."

"We didn't decide anything. You did. Just like you decide everything." Alyssa balled up her napkin and threw it on the table.

Carmen placed her hand on Trent's, stopping him before he could reply. She didn't want to see such a lovely evening turn ugly. "I don't mind answering. I didn't really date much."

"That's not an answer. How old were you?"

"You mean just me and my date alone? Or going out with a group?"

"Alone. Going out with a group isn't a real date."

"Okay. I was about twenty when I went on my first real date."

"Really?" Trent and Alyssa spoke at the same time.

"Yep." Carmen sighed. "I wasn't very popular when I was a teenager. Then I had some trouble at home and had to leave. I was busy doing other things, so I wasn't concerned about dating."

"You're no help," Alyssa said, slumping in her seat.

"Sorry."

"I bet twenty makes sixteen sound a lot better," Trent offered, stacking the empty plates.

"Not really," Alyssa murmured, taking the dishes into the kitchen. When she returned, she looked at Carmen. "Don't you think fourteen is old enough to date?"

"What I think doesn't matter. Your father gets to decide."

Alyssa crossed her arms over her chest. "Why?"

"Because he cares about you."

"Don't you care about me?"

"Of course I do. So do a lot of people. It would get really confusing if they all got a vote."

"Maybe. But Joni would totally agree with me."

"What about Uncle Lex?" Trent offered. "Maybe we should ask him."

"No way," Alyssa replied, wrinkling her nose. "He said you shouldn't let me date until I'm thirty."

"Then he definitely should get a vote."

"No. Just two people. Carmen, how old do you think I should be before I can date?"

"Sixteen."

"You're only saying that because Daddy did."

Carmen laughed but didn't deny it. Instead, she began to help clear the table. With four people working together, the food was put away and the dishwasher loaded.

"Now can I show Carmen my room?" Robyn asked. She'd clearly used up every drop of her patience.

Trent nodded.

Robyn grabbed Carmen's hand. "Wait until you see my princess bed."

Carmen was surprised when Alyssa joined them. She couldn't imagine Alyssa was as eager to show off her personal space.

Robyn's room was cute, if a little young for an eight-year-old. The walls were pink with a border of yellow daisies. There were framed pictures of nursery rhymes that were sweet, but more appropriate for a toddler. The furniture, though, was beautiful. There was a canopy bed that did indeed look fit for a princess, and a rocking chair with a baby doll sitting upright in the seat. Lace curtains billowing in the open window completed the effect.

Beside the bed was a framed photograph of a woman. Carmen easily guessed it was Anna. One quick glance revealed a smiling face. She was absolutely stunning. Carmen imagined Alyssa would look like her in a few years.

"Mommy decorated this room just for me," Robyn announced. "Do you like it?"

"It's very pretty."

Robyn smiled.

"Come see my room," Alyssa said, then crossed the hall and opened the door. "What do you think?"

Carmen stepped inside and looked around. The room was painted a sunny yellow with pink and green flowers. The furniture was identical to Robyn's. This was not at all what she expected. "Um..."

"I hate it. It looks like a little girl's room."

"Do you have an idea of what you would like instead?"

"I want to paint and I want new furniture."

"What color?"

"I don't know what color paint. I like a lot of colors. But I know I want cherry furniture."

"Are we painting our rooms?" Robyn asked hopefully. "Maybe we can do a big picture like you did at the youth center."

"That sounds good."

"There's only one problem," Alyssa said, frowning.

"What's that?"

"Daddy. He won't let us change anything in the whole house. So we need your help."

"How?" Carmen's stomach churned with tension.

"You have to ask him."

Carmen swallowed, imagining how she would even broach the subject with Trent. One thing was certain: it wouldn't be easy.

Chapter Sixteen

Trent lifted the top of the dessert box and smiled. Although he generally maintained a well-balanced diet, he had a weakness for sweets, especially chocolate. Polly's desserts were second to none and he stopped by the bakery at least once a week. He poured two glasses of milk and two mugs of coffee, then called Carmen and the girls for dessert.

He heard them whispering as they came down the stairs. Having a woman in the house changed his daughters for the better. Robyn and Alyssa liked Carmen and respected her opinion. She knew just what to say to defuse tough situations and had done so quite skillfully more than once today, turning what could have become an argument into a quiet discussion where everyone shared their opinion.

He liked having Carmen around. She was funny and witty and sexy as hell. She looked great in the shorts and top she had on at the youth center, but seeing her in that little red dress made his temperature rise. The dress wasn't especially revealing, but imagining what the fabric covered had him sweating. His libido had awakened with a vengeance from its seven-year slumber.

"Oh goody, cake!" Robyn exclaimed, sliding out her chair and sitting down so fast she nearly knocked it over and landed on her back. She grabbed her fork before Alyssa and Carmen even sat down.

"Hold your horses," Trent chided her gently. Table manners were something he hadn't focused on as much as he should.

Robyn grumbled but waited until everyone was seated before digging in. "We're playing Chutes and Ladders after dessert."

"Is that right?"

"Yep. Even Alyssa."

Trent glanced at his older daughter, who smiled and shrugged in return. Alyssa played with Robyn only when he wasn't around. Lately his presence killed her interest in games, and family fun night had long since gone by the wayside.

"Only a couple of games," Robyn said. "Then Carmen has to leave."

"And you have to take a bath," he reminded her.

After three rousing games of Chutes and Ladders, all of which Robyn won, Trent shooed her upstairs to the tub and Alyssa grabbed her phone and went to her room, no doubt to text Brooke for the next hour or so.

"Would you like more coffee?" Trent asked Carmen, reluctant to have the evening end. He hadn't realized how much he missed adult company. Not just adult company. Female company.

"No, thanks."

"I hope you don't need to rush off."

"Nope."

He took her elbow to lead her to the living room, but she pulled back slightly.

"It's a nice night and your porch swing is calling my name. Could we sit out there instead?"

"Sure."

"I love summer nights," she said, settling on the cushion with a contented sigh.

"Why is that?"

"There's just something magical about them."

She looked at him with such wonder in her eyes it touched his heart in a way it hadn't been touched in years. They were so close their thighs brushed. Hers was soft beneath the thin fabric of her dress. He could feel the gentle heat from her body, rising to mingle with his. She didn't wear much perfume, so he knew her enticing scent was unique to her. In that moment, with the last of the evening fading away and bright stars emerging in the darkening sky, he did indeed believe in magic.

She closed her eyes and leaned her head against the back of the swing, setting it into motion. Her hair caressed her shoulders and his fingers ached to touch it.

"When I was a little girl, I used to wish on stars." Her voice was soft, dreamy.

"Did any of your wishes come true?"

"Not that I remember."

The sadness in her voice had him reaching for her hand. "I'm sorry."

"It was a long time ago." She turned and smiled at him. "Did you wish on stars as a kid?"

"Nah." She was so close he could kiss her if he moved his head just an inch.

"Too girlie for you?"

"Too unrealistic. I never thought stars had supernatural powers."

"You wouldn't," she quipped, then lowered her voice as if sharing a well-guarded secret. "I never thought stars formed any type of pattern. I still don't. I think the constellations are just something the smart kids made up to make us other kids feel stupid."

"A giant conspiracy that has gone on for thousands of years?" He laughed. "No. They're real."

"You believe in the constellations?"

"I don't have to believe. I can see them."

He searched the sky and then pointed. "See that bright star?" She nodded hesitantly and he continued, "That's the North Star. Now follow the line down to the next brightest star and then around. If you look carefully, you'll see the Big Dipper and Ursa Major."

She squinted her eyes and tilted her head, her confusion sexier than it should be. She leaned her head over until her hair brushed against his cheek. It smelled sweeter than the flowers growing in his yard. Her closeness was arousing and he barely bit back a groan of desire. His impromptu astronomy lesson was beginning to feel more like foreplay.

"Do you really see something? Because all I see is a bunch of stars." She turned, and her lips nearly brushed his. Quickly glancing up at him, she stilled. The tip of her tongue darted out onto her bottom lip.

All rational thought fled his mind, taking with it the numerous reasons he couldn't get involved with Carmen. He gently touched her lips with his, giving her a chance to move away. He felt the answering pressure as her hands slid across his chest, leaving fire in their wake. Tilting his head for a better angle, he slanted his lips against hers, opened her mouth with his and slipped in his tongue.

She was sweeter than he imagined, tasting of coffee and

chocolate cake. The blood pounded in his veins, her touch heating it to near boiling. He wrapped his arms around her waist, pulling her closer to him, yet not close enough. She murmured his name against his lips, increasing his desire.

The sound of laughter followed by the slam of a car door jolted him, bringing him back to his surroundings. He was on his front porch, making out like a horny teenager. He eased back, reluctantly ending the kiss, then leaned his forehead against hers.

"Wow," she breathed, her voice soft and slightly shocked. "I didn't see that coming."

"Should I apologize?"

"Only for stopping."

"Nobody is sorrier for that than I am. But the chief of police shouldn't be caught making out in public."

She kissed him briefly before backing away. "It kind of kills the hard-nosed reputation, huh?"

"It doesn't help."

She leaned over and put on her shoes. He hadn't been aware she'd removed them. What else had escaped his attention while he let his desire get the best of him? "We need to talk."

"Not necessary." She brushed a slender finger over his wedding band. "I understand."

While he was trying to figure out what to say—heck, what he felt—Alyssa called his name. He and Carmen both jumped.

"Daddy," she said, bursting onto the porch. She stared at them and froze, whatever she intended to say forgotten for the moment. Her eyes narrowed with suspicion. "What's going on? What are you doing?"

"Your dad was trying to show me the constellations. I couldn't see them."

"Oh." Alyssa glanced over her shoulder. "There's the Little Dipper, Big Dipper and Ursa Major."

"Obviously I'm missing something," Carmen said with a chuckle. She rose and tucked her hair behind her ear. Trent tried not to stare, but it was the sexiest thing he'd seen in a long time. Maybe ever. "It's clear you and your dad need to talk. I'll go."

"You don't have to leave. It's not anything personal." Alyssa leaned against the rail and crossed her feet at the ankles. "I want to know if I can spend a couple nights with Brooke this week."

"I thought she was spending the summer with her father."

"She was. But it turns out he's getting married next week. Can you believe it?" she asked with total outrage. "And he just expected her to spend the summer with him and Candy."

"Candy being the new wife?"

Alyssa frowned. "I mean, get real. She told him she wanted to come home. At first he said no, but she said she'd hitchhike. He finally agreed, so she's flying home the day after tomorrow." Alyssa shook her head. "Can you believe he actually wanted her to come to the wedding? Like she would want to be there when her dad got married to some woman."

She straightened and pushed away from the banister. "Anyway, can I spend the night with her? I told her I'd ask and text her back."

"Sure. Just have her mom call me when everything is set."

"Okay." Alyssa dashed away happily, unaware of the ruins she'd left behind.

Carmen huffed out a breath. "I need to go."

Trent reached out, but she stepped back, dodging his hand.

"Thanks for dinner," she said. And then she was gone.

* * *

Carmen stared out the window of her room, not seeing the stars that flickered in the sky. Her hand brushed against her lips, still feeling the warmth from Trent's kiss. She'd been kissed before, but none had made her feel as if she might melt into a puddle. She'd never experienced a kiss so potent. A kiss that had left her oddly fulfilled, yet yearning for more.

If that contradictory thought didn't prove she was out of her mind, nothing would. And she certainly had to be out of her mind to kiss Trent Knight. The man was still in love with his wife. Carmen knew from pictures of her that the woman had been nothing short of spectacular. She'd possessed more than a beautiful face. Her eyes had been filled with compassion and laughter. Carmen had no doubt Anna Knight was a person she would have liked. No wonder Trent couldn't let her go.

Carmen had enjoyed her dinner with Trent. He was charming and funny and had kissed her so passionately she'd come out of her shoes. A few more seconds and she would have willingly come out of even more. She wanted to believe that he'd felt the same, but she could delude herself only so far. Sure, he'd enjoyed kissing her. That was physical. But she doubted his heart had been involved.

His heart was still filled with memories of his wife. As was his house. Carmen could tell he hadn't changed a thing. Every lamp, every pillow, every vase had been chosen by his late wife. And he'd left everything just the way she'd arranged it. As if he expected her to return at any time. His heart was still filled with her, so there was no room for Carmen.

And he still wore his wedding ring.

She moved away from the window, then closed the blinds on the night. She went into the attached bathroom and studied herself in the full-length mirror. She still wore her red dress. Though she'd returned to the B and B nearly forty minutes ago, she was reluctant to change. It was as if by not putting on her pajamas, the perfect evening was not over. She didn't want the night to end. Because despite everything, she had fallen in love with Trent Knight.

Chapter Seventeen

"Hey, Carmen," Alyssa said, walking into the art room. Next to her was another girl, the scowl on her face instantly noticeable. "This is my best friend, Brooke."

Carmen dropped the spray-painted macaroni onto a tray and smiled at the girl, who only rolled her eyes. Good grief, not another angst-filled teenager. Just how many lived in this small town? And how had she become the one designated to deal with them? She was going to suggest that Joni hire a counselor.

"Nice to meet you, Brooke. Are you interested in art?"

The girl glanced at the gold and silver pasta and shot Carmen a disbelieving stare. "I'll pass."

"We want to make jewelry. Is that all right?" Alyssa asked.

"Certainly. You know where everything is, so help yourself." Carmen turned to Brooke and plastered on another smile. "It was nice meeting you. Let me know if you need anything."

Alyssa's friend mumbled something as they walked away.

Carmen shook her head. Had she been as difficult as these girls at fourteen? All hormones and attitude? What was she thinking? She'd been the wild child of Sweet Briar. She'd been much worse.

Today one of the college girls was also volunteering, so Carmen headed to the break room. Joni was there and she held up a kettle. "Tea?"

"You must be the only person in the world who drinks tea when it's this hot. Even the devil is complaining."

"I fail to see what the temperature has to do with wanting a calming cup of tea. I just had a meeting with the town council and I need some chamomile." Joni filled the teakettle, set it on the stove and then dropped a teabag into a mug.

"That bad?"

"Worse. The old guard is still fighting Lex at every turn and I get caught in the cross fire." She waved her hand as if swatting away her exasperation. "Never mind that. I want to hear about your date with our oh-so-hot, but too-cool-to-sweat chief of police."

"How do you know about that?"

"You're kidding, right? This is Sweet Briar." Joni opened a bag of chocolate chip cookies and offered some to Carmen, who shook her head.

"Does Phil Henderson know his business is in jeopardy?" She pulled out a chair and joined Joni at the table. "This town doesn't need a newspaper when the gossip flows like water."

"True. So, how was it?"

"Nice. Good."

Joni frowned. "Nice is lunch with the pastor and his wife. Not dinner with Mr. Masculine."

"And his daughters."

"Oh. I guess that would be nice."

"Of course, we did sit on the porch alone."

"Was there kissing involved?"

Carmen felt her cheeks heat. "Some."

"That's the part I want to hear about. The romance."

To Carmen's horror, tears filled her eyes. She blinked them away, but it was too late. Joni had seen them. "What's wrong?"

"There is no romance."

Joni's lips curved in a knowing smile. "And you want one?"

"How stupid does that make me?"

"Why does that make you stupid? What's stupid about loving someone and wanting them to love you back?"

"Nothing. If that person actually does love you back. Everything if he doesn't."

"It's not stupid, regardless of whether the other person returns your feelings."

Carmen slumped in her seat. Realizing she was acting like a teenager, she sat up straight. "Have you ever been to Trent's house?"

"No. I never had a reason. Why?"

"He hasn't changed anything since his wife died."

"Maybe he's not much of a decorator. A lot of men don't care for that kind of thing." Joni rose and poured hot water into the mug and stirred in enough sugar to rot her teeth.

"It's not just that. I mean, I wouldn't expect him to go out and buy a whole houseful of new furniture. But something should be different."

"Did you ask him about it?"

"No," Carmen admitted.

"Here's your chance." Joni tilted her head. "He's right behind you."

Carmen turned as Trent entered the room, passing Joni

as she made a fast getaway. Despite Carmen's intention to protect her heart, she couldn't slow her suddenly racing pulse. He looked so handsome in his pressed uniform and spit-shined shoes. He stepped closer and his musky scent enveloped her. Any thought of asking about his home decor flew out the window. Who cared about that when she was caught in his simmering eyes? She swallowed hard. "What brings you here, Chief?"

He pursed his lips as though holding back a grin at her use of his title. His eyes sparkled with mischief. "Alyssa and Robyn have sleepovers tonight, so I'm here to pay my debt and ask you to dinner."

Vivid memories of their kiss had kept her awake all night, and she hoped for more. She tamped down her excitement by reminding herself he was asking her out only because of their bet. "We had dinner."

"That wasn't the date I promised you. I owe you a date at the finest restaurant around."

"Heaven on Earth?"

"Okay, the second finest restaurant around. I'd rather have dinner away from prying eyes."

"Is that possible?"

"Sure. If we leave town." He lifted his lips in a boyish grin. "You in?"

Despite herself, she nodded.

"I'll pick you up at six."

Then he was gone, leaving her humming with anticipation of the night to come.

Trent parked outside the B and B and inhaled deeply. The scent from the bouquet of mixed flowers filled his lungs and not for the first time he wondered if he was making a mistake. Was he betraying Anna? He hadn't dated anyone other than her; he hadn't been interested enough in another woman. Now his palms were sweating at the idea of seeing Carmen again.

His pulse picked up at the thought of kissing her at the end of the night. Her kiss had left him burning for more and he'd barely managed to keep from pulling her into his arms this afternoon. She'd looked so gorgeous, the simple top accenting her feminine curves, the denim skirt allowing teasingly brief glimpses of her long, slender legs.

Exiting the car, he climbed the steps in record time. Kristina Harrison, the owner of the B and B, welcomed him inside. Even though his back was to her, Trent knew the instant Carmen entered the room.

He turned, and numbness gripped his throat, making speech impossible. She looked ravishing in a turquoise dress that reduced him to a fifteen-year-old bumbling through his first date. He silently offered her the flowers, his pride growing when her look of surprise turned to delight.

"They're beautiful."

"I thought so until you walked into the room. Trust me, the flowers have nothing on you."

She laughed and brought the blossoms to her nose. "Are you going to flatter me all night?"

"That was the plan."

"That's a plan I can get behind."

She placed her flowers on a chair and handed him her shawl. Her dress was strapless and her honey skin glowed, tempting his fingers to linger. He hated the idea of covering one inch of her skin. Nevertheless he draped the soft fabric over her shoulders, wondering if he'd get the opportunity to remove it later.

She picked up the flowers. "I should ask for something to put these in."

Before the words were out of her mouth, Kristina was

back with a crystal vase. Promising to put the flowers in Carmen's room, she wished them both a good evening.

Trent offered Carmen his arm, then escorted her to his car.

"Where are we going?" she asked, as she fastened her seat belt.

"Giancarlo's. It's a new Italian restaurant in Willow Creek."

"Sounds wonderful." She leaned back and crossed her legs. Her frothy skirt rose, revealing well-toned thighs.

He swallowed hard and forced his attention back to the road. She sighed and his attention was once more drawn to her. "Everything okay?"

"I'm just enjoying the ride. It's been a long time since I've ridden on the back roads. I can't remember the last time I saw this many trees."

"Do you miss it?"

"Sweet Briar? Yes. I miss the weather. The slow pace. And the smell of the wildflowers and the ocean. Even the dirt smells different." She released a breath. "I guess I miss it more than I thought I did. Not that it matters."

"Why doesn't it matter?"

"Because I can't come home."

Because I can't come home. The words slipped out of Carmen's mouth before she could stop them. The longing was so clear that Trent couldn't have missed it. How could she have bared her soul so easily? She knew the answer. He was so easy to talk to. Somewhere along the way, he'd stopped judging her so harshly and had become a real friend. Other than Damon, she felt more comfortable with Trent than anyone else.

"Why not?"

"You were at the center. You heard Charlotte. My family doesn't want me back. I'm an embarrassment. The skeleton in the closet."

"I thought you weren't going to let their actions hurt you."

"I said I wasn't going to keep banging my head against a wall. But that doesn't mean their rejection doesn't hurt. It does."

He nodded. "It's their loss."

She hoped he would let the matter drop, and to her immense relief he did. They chatted about music and movies on the drive, laughing when they discovered they had total opposite tastes.

As they entered the restaurant, wonderful aromas floated on the air, making her mouth water. A hostess led them to a candlelit table near a window. Trent held her chair and the heat from his body sent shivers down her spine.

"Everything here tastes great," he said, taking his seat.

She nodded, but with the way her blood sizzled in her veins, she doubted she would taste even the most delicious fare. As if he sensed her nerves, he became more talkative, captivating her with funny stories of what he referred to as his misspent youth.

This night was one of the best she'd had in more years than she could count. Time flew and much too soon they were driving back to Sweet Briar. She recognized the area where he'd pulled her over for speeding. So much had changed in such a short time.

"I can take you back to the B and B, or we can have a nightcap at my place."

Carmen's heart stuttered and her breath caught in her throat. She knew what he was suggesting. Or at least she thought she did. She dared a glance at him, taking in his strong and honest profile. She expelled the breath she'd been holding. "That sounds nice."

At the stoplight, he turned away from the B and B and toward his home. Her heart was pounding in her throat as he parked. He opened his door, crossed in front of the car and opened hers. It seemed so natural to leave her hand in his even after he'd helped her exit the car.

A breeze blew, cooling her skin, and she gathered her shawl more closely.

"Cold?" Trent asked. He'd removed his suit jacket earlier and now he slipped it over her shoulders. The fabric retained his familiar scent, which floated up to her nostrils.

"Thanks." They climbed the steps in silence. "Do you mind sitting on the swing for a bit?"

"Nope. I have a fond memory from the last time we sat here together."

"Careful, Chief," she said, as his arm came around her shoulders and the swing began to gently glide. "You don't want to get caught necking like a teenager. You do have an image to uphold."

"I don't see how stealing kisses from the prettiest girl in town ruins my image. If anything, being with you is improving my image."

She leaned her head against his shoulder. "That's the nicest thing anyone has ever said to me."

"Then you need to start hanging out with people who see you the way I do."

Her heart skipped. She was so touched she could barely speak above a hopeful whisper. "How do you see me?"

He stroked her hair, gently pulling his hands through the curly locks. "When I look at you, I see a strong woman. A woman handed some of the worst life can give, but who thrived. You're compassionate and loving. You managed to reach my daughter when I couldn't. When I look at you, I see a woman I admire. A woman I'm longing to kiss."

The last words were spoken seconds before his lips brushed hers.

The kiss they'd shared the other night had been tentative. Exploratory and sweet. This kiss, while no less gentle, was more assured. More passionate. Breathing hard, Trent broke the kiss and leaned his forehead against hers. "You make me forget myself. I can't think straight when we're together."

"Why do you need to think?"

"Beats me." He brushed his thumb over her bottom lip. "It's getting late. Should I take you back to the B and B, or would you like to stay here? With me."

"You mean have our own sleepover?"

He lifted her hand to his lips and kissed her knuckles. "Mmm-hmm. Although I can't guarantee you'll get much sleep."

Her blood heated as much from his words as from his touch. Wondering if she was making the biggest mistake of her life, she stood. "I'd love to stay."

Chapter Eighteen

Trent lay in the dark listening to Carmen's even breathing. She was curled next to him, her head on his shoulder, her soft hand on his bare chest as she slept. He wasn't surprised to discover she was a generous lover. She had a giving nature. What had been unexpected was her shyness. She'd seemed almost unsure. That made two of them. He was in way over his head.

He hadn't expected the depth of emotion he'd felt, the connection with a woman he hadn't known very long. The sense of belonging together had shocked him. He hadn't been using Carmen to scratch an itch. He'd never do that. But the level of caring and sharing between them, the feeling of rightness, had been a surprise. He wasn't sure how he felt about it.

Leaves rustled in the breeze and an owl hooted outside his open window. A cloud floated by, momentarily blocking the moonlight. Carmen stirred and slid closer.

He cuddled her and closed his eyes. He'd think about the night and what it meant in the morning. Right now he was too content to do anything other than sleep.

A few minutes later, someone was shaking his shoulder. "What?" he growled, pulling a pillow over his face. He inhaled Carmen's familiar scent and was filled with desire. Despite being drowsy, his blood began pounding through his veins. He reached for Carmen but found only cooling sheets.

"It's late. I need to get going."

He opened his eyes. Carmen was fully dressed and sitting on the edge of his bed. "What time is it?"

"Almost four. You were sleeping so peacefully, I hate waking you, but this is Sweet Briar. If I go waltzing into the B and B in a couple hours wearing these clothes, it'll be all over town before sunrise. Neither sleet nor snow nor dark of night shall keep the busybodies from wagging their tongues."

He frowned. She had a point. There was no privacy in this town. While it was no one's business whom he chose to take to bed, he didn't want his sex life to be the featured special at the diner for the next week.

Not only that, he wasn't sure how Alyssa would react if she knew he'd spent the night with Carmen. She'd been angry on Brooke's behalf because her friend's father was remarrying. She might feel the same way about him being linked with a woman. Though she liked Carmen, Alyssa might not accept her in his life. His relationship with his daughter was difficult enough. He couldn't risk making it worse.

After stretching, he threw off the sheet and sat up. The wind blew the curtain and a shaft of moonlight illuminated the room. He couldn't remember the last time he'd slept that well. After rubbing a hand down his face in a futile attempt to wipe away the sleep, he yawned and gave his head a hard shake. Man, he could use some coffee. "Give me five minutes."

Carmen grew still. Her smile froze, then faded. She averted her gaze. "I'll meet you downstairs."

What was that about? Maybe she was worried about the busybodies. She'd been the subject of enough gossip to last two lifetimes.

He reminded himself of that fact ten minutes later when he parked in front of the Victorian. She'd been quiet the entire drive, twisting the fabric of her dress. In fact, she'd barely spoken to him from the time he'd come downstairs. She seemed uncomfortable, but for the life of him he didn't know why. He expelled a breath. He didn't know the morning-after dance. He'd never performed it. He didn't like it.

He opened his door. She put her hand on his arm and he looked up.

"You don't have to get out. It's only a few steps."

"No. I'll walk you to the door." She opened her mouth and he cut short her protest. "No arguments."

She frowned, then nodded.

He circled the car and helped her out. She didn't hold on to his hand the way she had the night before, but instead dropped it as soon as she'd risen from the vehicle. It was as if she was deliberately creating distance between them. But why? She'd been fine last night. Better than fine. And she'd been smiling when she woke him this morning.

He searched his mind but couldn't think of anything he'd said or done that she might have taken the wrong way. Maybe she expected him to say or do something more. He groaned. He had no idea what she expected. It was too early in the morning to have a deep conversation. Not that she showed any interest in talking.

When they reached the door, she turned and looked somewhere in the vicinity of his hairline. "Thanks. I had a great time."

"So did I." Before he could make a move to kiss her, or even decide if it was a good idea, she was inside and behind the closed door. Well, that was certainly clear, if nothing else was. He shoved his hands into his pockets and trudged to his car, wondering what in the hell had happened.

Carmen managed to make it to her room and close the door before collapsing on the bed. What had she been thinking? She'd had sex with Trent. Twice. Not that there was anything wrong with that in theory. Or in practice, for that matter. Trent was a thorough and gentle lover and he'd shown her a level of pleasure she hadn't known existed. She'd felt so comfortable in his arms. All had been right in her world. Physically, she'd been in heaven. But when he rubbed his hand down his face after she awakened him, the moon glinted off his ring, plunging her into hell.

How could she have forgotten about the wedding ring the man still wore? The ring signifying his unending commitment to another woman. The ring signifying he was not emotionally available to her.

He was charming and funny and seemed so into her that she forgot his heart belonged to another woman. She'd gotten swept up in the romantic moment like some fictional princess and had turned off her brain. No part of her life resembled a fairy tale, so why did she expect Trent to return her feelings like a prince caught under a spell? She didn't know why he'd had sex with her, but doubted it was because he'd fallen in love with her.

Well, what was done was done. She'd made enough mistakes in her life to know that the past couldn't be changed, only accepted, so she wouldn't beat herself up over it. She just wouldn't repeat the mistake.

Trent reviewed the arrest report submitted by the department's newest officer, signed it and put it in the out basket. He hated paperwork, but it was a big part of the job. Picking up his World's Greatest Dad mug, he took an unsatisfying swallow of coffee that had long since gone cold, walked to the window and stared at the town.

Old Man Smith was sitting outside his barbershop, puffing on the one cigar his wife allowed him each week. Ernie Peters and Bob Jackson were at a table beside him, playing checkers and no doubt reminiscing about the good old days. Several tourists walked by carrying bags from one of the new exclusive boutiques that had sprouted up over the past few years.

"I'm going on patrol and then to lunch," he announced to his dispatcher Ella.

"Stopping by the youth center?"

He froze, wondering if there was a hint of gossip in her voice. He met her eyes. They were open and as honest as she was. "I hadn't planned to."

"I thought you went by to see your daughters every day."

"Usually. But Robyn is spending the day at the amusement park with a friend. Alyssa is hanging out with Brooke." So at a time he wanted to see Carmen the most, he had no excuse to drop by. He could just go in and see her, but that would attract unwanted attention. Besides, the last time they'd been together, she'd raced away from him. He'd wait awhile before trying to figure out what was bothering her.

He drove the city streets, then, satisfied that all was quiet, parked in front of the diner. As usual, it was crowded, but luckily, most of the customers seemed to be wrapping up. He could eat at the station, but he enjoyed his meals more when he wasn't answering the phone and dealing with various problems.

He grabbed an empty table and signaled to a waitress, who brought over a menu that he waved away. "I'll have the meat loaf special with extra gravy on the mashed potatoes, and iced tea."

She scribbled his order on a pad and promised to return with his drink. As she went back to the kitchen, the bell tinkled over the door and Carmen walked in.

His pulse picked up at the sight of her in a pink top and a flowered skirt that stopped a few inches above her knees, showcasing her world-class legs. She caught sight of him and her eyes sparkled briefly before dimming. What was that about?

He considered waiting until they had more privacy to talk, but he couldn't. Last night had been the best night in years. He thought she'd felt the same. But something had gone wrong. Did she regret making love with him? Was she embarrassed? Unsure? What?

Rising, he closed the distance between them. To her credit, she didn't turn or pretend she hadn't seen him. That was good. Maybe he could find out what was wrong.

"Hi," he said, when they were close enough to speak. He inhaled her intoxicating scent and was immediately transported to last night when he'd had her in his arms. Blood began racing through his veins and he told himself to calm down. "Want to join me? I just ordered."

She shook her head. "I'm picking up an order to go."

A waitress returned with a large brown paper bag and gave it to Carmen, who handed over a wad of cash before looking back at him. "I'll see you around."

He put a hand on her arm. "Help me out here. Did I do something wrong?"

"No."

"Then why the cold shoulder?"

She looked around the room. They had attracted the attention of several patrons. "I need to get back. People are waiting for their food."

"Five minutes," he said, not wanting to plead, but pleading anyway. Something was off. He needed to get things settled before it was too late.

She looked at him, then nodded.

He led her out the door and away from prying eyes. "I'm trying to figure out what I did wrong. Did I hurt you last night?"

That seemed to take her aback and her eyes widened. "No. You were wonderful."

"Then why the distance?" She opened her mouth and he raised a hand, cutting her off. "And don't say it's my imagination."

"I wasn't going to say that. I wasn't sure how you felt or if you..."

"If I what?"

"If you regretted it."

"Why would you think that?"

"It's not something we planned. You might want to forget it ever happened."

Guilt pummeled him and he wondered if she would have had those doubts if he hadn't been so cruel to her initially. His feelings had changed, but she didn't know just how much. Still, he had a sense there was more she wasn't saying. "How about I come around this evening and we can talk things out."

She hesitated a moment as if she was debating. Finally, she nodded, and relief flooded him.

"Okay. I'll come around eight." And between now and then he had to come up with a plan to get things back on track.

Carmen ran a comb through her hair, grabbed her purse and headed downstairs. She'd changed into white shorts and a peach top. When she reached the front room, she wasn't surprised to see Trent waiting. He'd changed into jeans that molded his powerful thighs and a navy T-shirt that stretched tight across his massive chest and shoulders. Despite the fact that she wanted to distance herself from the train that threatened to run over her heart, she felt herself smiling at the sight of him.

He took her hand and gently kissed her cheek, weakening her knees. Maybe he did care about her. Perhaps guided by the need to protect her heart, she'd run away too soon. But how could she build a happy future with Trent knowing that she'd played a role in his wife's death? And given their pasts, would he truly be able to forgive her or love her the way he'd loved Anna?

Despite the doubts swirling around inside her, when he smiled at her, a seed of hope planted itself in her heart.

"I thought we might take a walk on the beach. I know how much you like it."

They didn't speak as they walked. A refreshing breeze blew, stirring the beach grass. As they neared the ocean, the smell of salt filled the air. Carmen inhaled deeply, then sighed. "I love the way it smells out here."

"Like home?"

Surprised, she spun to face him. "How did you know?"

"I feel the same way."

There was a faint sound of music that grew louder as they stepped onto the sand. Laughter mingled with the pounding bass and screeching guitar. "Sounds like a party."

His expression was grim as he reached for his cell phone.

"What are you doing?" she asked, placing a hand on his forearm.

"Calling an officer."

"Why? It's a public beach. Curfew is not for hours."

"Underage drinking is illegal."

"You don't know they are drinking. Don't you think you should give them the benefit of the doubt? Or at least see for yourself what's happening before calling someone?"

He stared at her so long she thought he might brush off her hand and place his call. Finally, he nodded. "You're right. I automatically jumped to a conclusion."

"Old habits and all that."

They followed the noise to a group of about twenty teens. Some were dancing and others were sitting in a circle around a cooler, laughing and talking. Flattened soda cans were piled on a stack of empty pizza boxes. One of the girls glanced up and noticed them. She poked the person beside her. Within a minute everyone was staring at Trent and Carmen.

Finally, Carmen broke the uneasy silence. "We don't mean to intrude. We're just passing by."

"Right," Trent added. "We know there's no underage drinking going on."

"That's right." One of the teens opened the cooler and tilted it in Trent's direction. He moved the cans around in the melting ice. "See. Only soda, Chief."

Trent smiled. "As you were."

They walked away with the sound of merriment behind them. Three girls in swimsuits emerged from the water and ran toward the others.

"Brooke?" Trent's voice was a mixture of surprise and anger.

The teens stopped. Alyssa's best friend told the other girls to go without her, then stared at Trent. She folded her arms across her chest.

Trent strode across the sand, while Carmen followed more slowly. This wasn't going to be pretty. "What are you doing here?"

The girl rolled her eyes. "It's a party."

"Where's Alyssa?"

The girl's eyes darted toward a sand dune and then back to Trent. She shrugged.

Eyes narrowed, Trent stalked in that direction. His hands were fisted and he practically vibrated with anger. Carmen raced to keep up, cursing the sand as she slipped.

"Calm down," she said, grabbing at his hand.

He yanked it away. "Don't tell me to calm down."

"Don't do anything rash."

He ignored her.

Shaking her head, she bit back more words she knew he wouldn't listen to, then barreled into him when he stopped suddenly. Fearing the worst, she put a hand on his shoulder and peered around him, then released a relieved breath. Alyssa and Joseph were sitting close together, her head on his shoulder, his arm around her waist. He leaned in and brushed her lips with his. Trent's already stiff spine became like hardened steel.

"Get away from my daughter."

Alyssa and Joseph sprang apart. Joseph jumped to his feet, then helped Alyssa to stand. He looked at Trent and Carmen with a puzzled frown. "What's wrong?"

"What's wrong is your hands are on my daughter."

"Daddy," Alyssa began.

"Don't say a word, Alyssa. I'm so disappointed in you."

"For what?"

"Sneaking out."

"I didn't sneak out. Mrs. Banks knows where I am. You can call and ask her. We have to be back by nine thirty."

"You didn't mention a party when we talked this morning."

Joseph stepped forward, deftly placing himself in front of Alyssa. "I only invited her a few hours ago, sir."

"I'm talking to my daughter."

"You're yelling at her. If you want to be angry, be angry at me."

"I am. You're making out with my fourteen-year-old daughter."

"We weren't making out—"

"I just kissed her."

"Hold on," Carmen said, hoping to keep the situation from becoming even more explosive.

"Don't interfere. This is a family matter. I can handle it without your help," Trent snapped, his face an angry mask, his voice clipped. Dismissive. As if he hadn't asked her to remain in town in order to help him rebuild his crumbling relationship with Alyssa.

Carmen swallowed the anger and hurt that surged through her. Trent was right. This was a family matter and she had no part in it. But she cared about both of them. She didn't want him to say words in anger that could become an impenetrable barrier destroying the bond between father and daughter. Painful words that would burn a hole in Alyssa's soul that would last for years and years. Carmen could feel the tension radiating through his body, so she didn't think he had enough self-control to watch what he said. "I'm sure you can. But you should calm down before you say something you'll regret."

Again he ignored her. He pointed a finger at his daughter. "You're too young to even think about having a boyfriend."

Alyssa stepped around Joseph, who once again moved between her and her father as if to protect her. "How can you be such a hypocrite? All my life you've told me how you and Mom fell in love in sixth grade. You guys were only eleven years old."

"That's different. What your mother and I experienced was special. A love like that is a once-in-a-lifetime thing."

Carmen felt her heart crack and looked at her shirt, half expecting to see blood. Of course, there was none. Surprisingly, no one else heard her heart breaking and they continued to argue.

She'd been deluding herself. Trent would never open his heart to her. It belonged to Anna and always would.

Chapter Nineteen

"I love Alyssa." Joseph reached for Alyssa's hand, which she gave him without a hint of hesitation.

"And I love Joseph," she said, staring into the young man's eyes. Then she turned and faced Trent, lifting her chin defiantly, silently daring him to scoff at her feelings.

He bit back harsh words. Carmen was right. He didn't want to ruin his relationship with his daughter, but he couldn't stand quietly by and watch this train wreck occur. One hormone-driven moment could ruin Alyssa's life. He wouldn't be much of a father if he didn't try to stop her from making a huge mistake. What was he supposed to say in the face of these declarations? No doubt Alyssa believed she was in love. She was fourteen, after all. She'd probably fall in love with a different boy every week. Trent wasn't as sure about Joseph's sincerity. Seventeen-year-old boys were notorious for not knowing the difference between love and lust, and not caring to find out.

"Carmen?" Trent said, turning in her direction.

"You're right. It's not my business. I'm going to leave and let you all work this out." She backed away, turned and headed farther down the beach.

Suddenly, Trent wasn't sure he could handle this on his own. Maybe he did need Carmen's input. Alyssa might be more willing to listen to a woman than to him. "Wait."

She stopped but otherwise didn't move, leaving him to close the distance between them. He'd been so focused on Alyssa, he hadn't been paying attention to Carmen. For the first time he noted her stricken face.

She looked everywhere but at him. He shouldn't have spoken so harshly. She'd only been trying to help and he'd bitten her head off. Carmen had separated herself from him emotionally as well as physically. Not that he could blame her. Was he ever going to get it right? Regret for what he'd said to her and fear for Alyssa roiled his stomach.

"I need your help. I don't know how to reach her. I've got to help her see the mistake she's making."

Shaking her head, Carmen held up her hands, palms toward him. "You were right. This is something the two of you should handle without outside interference."

He reached for her, but she put her hands behind her back. "I need to go," she said softly.

Feeling helpless, he watched as she turned and hurried across the beach, as if she couldn't get away from him fast enough. She didn't look back once. He'd blown it. He'd hurt her. Despite the strong urge to follow and beg her forgiveness, he turned back to the young lovers. He was not about to leave them to their own devices. He'd seen enough to know what they might get up to if left alone.

Taking a calming breath, he went back to where the teens stood, their hands still clasped, presenting a unified front. *Don't overreact.* "Alyssa, we need to talk. I'll call

Mrs. Banks and let her know I'm taking you home. We'll see if she wants us to drop Brooke off at their house."

Alyssa glared, sending daggers shooting in his direction.

Joseph turned and cupped her face. "Will you be all right?"

"Of course she'll be all right," Trent said, his temper flaring again. He didn't like what the kid was implying. He'd never laid a hand on either of his daughters.

Joseph didn't take his eyes off Alyssa. And didn't acknowledge Trent's words.

She smiled gently and placed her hand on Joseph's. "I'll be fine."

He stood unmoving for a few seconds, as if considering her answer. Apparently satisfied, he dropped his hand. "I'll call you later."

"Alyssa won't be receiving phone calls tonight."

For a minute Trent thought the kid was going to argue, but instead he inclined his head and walked away. Unlike Carmen, he looked back several times.

Alyssa folded her arms against her chest, mutiny in her expression. No doubt she was gearing up for one heck of a fight. Again, he wished he'd accepted Carmen's offer of help. In the space of only a few weeks, she'd formed a rapport with his daughter that he didn't have.

Turning away from her fury, he called Mrs. Banks, who assured him, with some annoyance, she did indeed know where the girls were and that she would pick up Brooke.

Was he out of touch? Overprotective? No. He'd seen dangers others chose to pretend didn't exist. He had to protect his daughter.

"Satisfied?" she snarled, when he ended the call.

"Not really. Let's go."

She huffed but followed him across the beach to the

car. When they were seated, she turned her back to him and stared out the passenger window. Fine. He could do the silent treatment, too. Switching on the radio to a jazz station he knew she hated, he pulled into the street and took the long way home. Immature? Probably, but he was just as unhappy with her as she was with him. Besides, he needed the time to cool off and get his thoughts together.

"I have nothing to say to you," Alyssa yelled as soon as they stepped into the house. She crossed her arms and tried to stare him down.

Calm down before you say something you'll regret. He exhaled. One of them had to be mature, and as the parent, that role fell to him. "Then listen while I talk to you."

"Do I have a choice?"

He ignored the sarcasm and nodded, pretending the question had been sincerely asked. He pointed to a chair and indicated she should sit. She blew out an exasperated breath, then made a great show of stomping across the room and dropping into the chair farthest away from him. For good measure, she moved it back another foot. He heaved a heavy sigh as he sat down.

Since inspiration hadn't hit, he decided to go with his heart. He leaned forward, elbows on his knees, his hands hanging free. "I love you, Alyssa. You and your sister mean more to me than anything in the world."

Her eyes widened in surprise, then filled with tears, which she blinked away. Her lips curled in a sneer. "Since when?"

"Since forever. Since the day you were born and I held you in my arms for the first time. No. Before then. I loved you from the moment your mother told me she was pregnant. I knew that second that I'd love you forever."

Alyssa was silent, considering his words. Her body lost some of its stiffness, although her arms remained folded.

He forced himself not to say more. She needed time to think about what he'd told her. Eventually, she looked up. "If you love me, then why did you embarrass me?"

"It wasn't my intention."

"You accused me of sneaking around. I've never done that in my life."

"I'm sorry. I was wrong. You've always been honest. You didn't deserve that."

"So why did you?" Her voice was quiet. Pained.

He exhaled. "I panicked. You're my little girl and I hate seeing you make a mistake."

"I'm not a little girl. And I'm not making a mistake. I love Joseph and he loves me."

Trent wanted to pace but made himself stay seated. "You think you're in love."

"I know I'm in love."

"You don't even know the boy."

"You're wrong. You're the one who doesn't know him. That's why you don't like him. But if you knew Joseph, you would. Then you'd know that I'm right and that he loves me."

Trent rubbed the back of his neck, wishing like heck she would listen but knowing she wouldn't. "Okay. Tell me about Joseph."

Alyssa sighed and smiled softly. Her eyes lit with warmth from within. "He's nice and he cares about me. Remember when nobody would talk to me? He made them stop ignoring me. Then he introduced me to his friends. They're as nice as he is. Now all the kids who were being mean want to hang out with me again, but I don't want to. They weren't really my friends. Now I have people I can count on. Like Joseph."

"That was good of him."

"That's just the way he is. He's cool, but he's not a jerk

like a lot of cool kids. Plus he's so talented. You saw what he did to the mural at the youth center."

Trent stifled a groan. Yeah, he'd seen. Graffiti. "He's a good artist, Alyssa. But you're both young. You might be confusing what you feel. Joseph made everyone stop mistreating you. You're grateful. That's normal. I'm grateful, too. But you might be mistaking gratitude for love."

She shook her head, her lips compressed. "I'm not stupid. I know the difference."

"Getting your feelings confused doesn't make you stupid. Anybody can do that. Even Joseph."

"Now you're saying Joseph doesn't love me? That he's just confused? I haven't done anything for him, so he can't be confusing gratitude with love."

Trent had to be careful here. "No. But he might be confusing love with lust."

Her head jerked up. "Why don't you just say what you mean? You think Joseph is only pretending to love me so I'll have sex with him. Well, you're wrong. He loves me and I love him. But I hate you."

She jumped to her feet and ran from the room. A minute later her door slammed so hard the windows rattled.

Feeling more despair than he had in a while, Trent slumped in his chair. It wasn't supposed to be this hard. He'd known this day was coming and foolishly thought he'd be ready to handle it. Maybe he'd do better tackling the problem with the other woman in his life.

He reared back. Where had that come from? Did he just think of Carmen as the woman in his life? They were friends. Friends with benefits? He hated that phrase. Either you were friends or you were lovers and in a relationship. There was no in-between. So why had he made love with her? He didn't believe it was a matter of desire getting the best of him. And he knew it wasn't love. So what was it? He didn't know.

But what he did know was that it would be unfair to make love with her again no matter how desperately he wanted to. He had to make sure she understood that although he did not have regrets, they wouldn't be making love again.

Fortunately, Carmen was an adult and wouldn't make the mistake of thinking making love meant they were in love. He had no doubt she would understand. Now that he thought about it, she'd attempted to put distance between them and he was the one who'd resisted. Perhaps she already realized they'd made a mistake. Regardless, he still owed her an apology for his behavior today. Once he apologized, he'd make sure they were on the same page regarding their relationship.

He grabbed his keys and hollered up to Alyssa that he was going out. Silence was the only response. Hopefully, things would go better with Carmen.

Carmen stared up at the moonlit sky. A handful of stars twinkled and more joined in every minute. Was it only a couple nights ago that Trent had tried to point out the constellations to her? It seemed like forever. Maybe time stretched and contracted when you had a broken heart.

She couldn't blame Trent for her pain. She'd known he was still in love with Anna when she made love with him. Perhaps his own broken heart had made time stand still, freezing him seven years ago. At least it appeared that way to her.

The temperature had dropped and a slight chill filled the air. She rubbed her arms, then wrapped them around her knees. If only she had brought her sweater. The kids had ended their party and she was alone on the beach. She wasn't ready to trade in the soothing sound of the waves lapping the shore for the deafening silence of her room at the B and B.

A car door closed in the distance and she hoped her solitude wasn't about to be disturbed. A moment later she heard her name being called and realized she wasn't going to get her wish.

"I thought I'd find you here," Trent said. He sat down, not waiting for an invitation.

She glanced over at him, then back at the water.

"Cold?"

"Maybe a little bit."

He shrugged out of his windbreaker and wrapped it around her. The jacket was still warm from his body and it felt somehow intimate. His musky scent surrounded her, bringing back memories of their night together. She shoved them into a dark corner of her mind, determined they'd never see the light of day again.

"Thanks."

They watched the waves roll onto the shore in silence. Finally, she spoke. "How'd it go with Alyssa?"

"Not well. She says she hates me."

Despite her vow to keep her distance, Carmen's heart ached for him. "You know she doesn't mean it, right?"

"At this point, I don't know anything."

He looked so depressed. She grabbed his hand and squeezed it. "I've been around Alyssa for a while and I know for sure she loves her daddy. You're her hero."

"She's making a big mistake, but she won't listen to me."

"How do you know it's a mistake?"

"She's fourteen."

"That's it? That's your entire argument?" Carmen picked up one of the dozen or so seashells she'd piled beside her and placed it on her lap. This time when she left she'd take a piece of home with her to combat the loneliness of the crowded city. It might be her last chance, because she didn't know if she would ever return. She and her family still had not reconciled and she didn't think they ever would.

"She's too young to know what love is." He held up his hand as if to forestall any argument Carmen might have. "That's not why I came to find you."

"You were looking for me?" Despite everything, her heart leaped in her chest and hope blossomed. Fortunately, her voice didn't reflect her feelings. "Why?"

"To apologize. You were trying to help with Alyssa and I bit your head off."

"You were upset."

"Yes, but I was also an idiot. You're a good friend and I treated you poorly. Please forgive me."

Friend. She was a good friend. Trent was a smart man. He may have misspoken while talking with his daughter because he was upset. He was calm now. Collected. She had no doubt he'd chosen his words with great deliberation. He was sending her a message. She was his friend. Only his friend.

The hope in her heart withered, but she lifted her chin. He'd never know how much she wanted him to return her feelings. As if in sympathy with her pain, a cloud floated past the moon, temporarily hiding its light.

She pasted a tight smile on her face even though she wasn't sure he could see it. "Of course I forgive you. I know you were worried. Besides, as you said, we're friends."

"Thanks."

"If that's all, I need to get back to my room."

He placed a hand on her arm. Even through the fabric of his jacket, and regardless of the ache in her heart, her body still responded to the contact. "No, that's not all." He released her arm. "I need to apologize for what happened between us."

"Excuse me?"

"I feel bad, like I took advantage of you. I'm sorry."

"You're sorry? That we made love?" She couldn't do this. Not now when her dashed hopes lay between them.

"Carmen—"

"Your apology isn't necessary."

"I didn't want you to get the wrong idea."

"You mean like thinking that you're in love with me? I'm not fourteen. I know the difference between love and lust. Trust me. That thought never crossed my mind." Too bad saying it out loud didn't make it true.

"That's not what I meant."

"Then what?" She hoped he was quick before her bravado ran out and she burst into tears. As it was, her eyes were beginning to burn.

His were filled with sincerity. "I don't want you to think of me as the kind of man who would take advantage of you. That I'm the type who would use you for my own pleasure."

If he had no feelings for her, that was exactly what he'd done. But she'd wanted him, too, just for a different reason. She didn't know how to answer him, so she didn't try.

He dropped his head. "What happened…that's never… I haven't been with a woman besides Anna."

He looked at Carmen and she nodded. She didn't realize a tear had fallen until he brushed it away with his thumb. She drew back from his touch.

"If I could love anyone else, it would be you."

The tears began to fall in earnest. She pushed to her feet. "I have to go."

"Carmen, I'm so sorry. I've hurt you. I never meant to do that."

He reached for her, but she dodged his hands. Nothing he could say would take the hurt away. "I know."

She ran across the beach away from Trent, wishing she could escape the pain in her heart as easily.

Chapter Twenty

"I'm coming," Trent yelled to whoever was pounding on his front door. At first, he'd thought ignoring the doorbell would make the soon-to-be-sorry idiot now banging on his door go away. Apparently, this jerk didn't know he was taking his life into his hands.

Trent felt like crap. It was as if a jackhammer were blasting away in his head. He rubbed his hand over his brows, hoping to remove the ache. The physical pains were nothing compared with the emotional ones. Not only was Alyssa making a big production of ignoring him, but he'd hurt Carmen.

A few weeks ago, the thought of her suffering would have given him pleasure. Now remembering the silent tears running down her cheeks last night was enough to bring him to his knees. He never should have touched her. When he found himself coming to care for her, his desire increasing, he should have backed off. If he had, she wouldn't be hurting now.

The doorbell pealed again, followed by more pounding.

"What?" he growled, as he swung the door open.

Joseph stood on the porch, his jaw set with determination. Great.

"I want to see Alyssa."

"No. Now go away." Trent started to close the door, but the teen blocked it with his foot.

"I'm not going away until I see her."

Trent stepped outside, pulling the door closed behind him. "You do realize I'm the chief of police."

To his credit, the youth stood taller and threw back his shoulders. He even took a step closer to Trent. "Yes. And do you realize I'm not leaving until I see Alyssa?"

Trent wasn't sure whether to be angry or amused. "Maybe I wasn't clear yesterday. You are too old to date my daughter. She won't be entertaining you in our home."

"She wasn't at the youth center today."

"That was her choice."

"So you say. But I'm not leaving until I see her."

"Listen, son," Trent began.

Joseph stiffened and his eyes blazed. "I'm not your son."

"It's just a figure of speech." Trent acknowledged Joseph might have been justifiably annoyed by his condescending tone, but being called son was not something that should have angered the teen. Trent studied the young man before him. Beneath the anger he saw concern and...fear. But not for himself.

Trent thought back to last night and the way Joseph kept putting himself between Trent and Alyssa, as if to protect her from a blow. Then there was his insistence now that he see Alyssa. Trent considered everything he knew about Joseph. He was the son of a single woman. Either his father or some other male in his life had abused his mother. No doubt the youth had tried to protect her. There were probably some holes in his theory, but Trent believed he had the basics correct. One thing was sure: unless Trent physically removed him, Joseph wasn't leaving until he saw for himself that Alyssa was fine.

Trent opened the door and stepped inside, holding it open. Joseph's eyes widened as he realized he'd gained admittance to the house. He rushed in as if fearful Trent would change his mind.

"Wait here. She's in her room."

Trent took the stairs two at a time, all the while wondering if he'd lost his mind. He should be doing everything in his power to discourage a relationship between Alyssa and Joseph, yet here he was, bringing the two of them together. But he couldn't in good conscience leave Joseph wondering about Alyssa. And it wouldn't hurt for her to have a friend in her corner willing to go toe-to-toe with anyone, including her own father, to assure her safety. He couldn't ask for more than that. As long as they were just friends.

He knocked on her closed door. "Alyssa."

"Go away. I'm not talking to you."

Yeah. He'd figured that out two hours ago when she didn't eat her breakfast. He'd made all her favorites, but she chose to eat cold cereal straight out of the box instead. He'd deliberately left her untouched plate on the table, but she didn't sneak one bite. She took stubborn to a whole new level.

Wonder where she got that?

"There's someone here to see you."

"Who?"

"Joseph."

She snorted. "Yeah, right. Like you'd actually let him in the house."

"It's true, Alyssa," Joseph said.

Apparently unwilling to wait, he'd followed Trent upstairs and was standing a couple feet away. If not for the visible concern on the youngster's face, Trent would have sent him downstairs.

"Joseph?" Alyssa's voice was filled with surprise. The sound of scrambling and bumping came through the door. "I'll be right down."

"Why don't you open the door?" Joseph asked.

"Because she needs to comb her hair and change out of her grungy pajamas," Trent said.

"They're not grungy," said the disgruntled voice behind the door. "But go downstairs. I need to wash up."

"Come on, Joseph," Trent said, starting down the stairs. He felt almost kindly toward the kid. Alyssa had actually spoken to him.

"What's taking her so long?" Joseph asked when they'd been in the living room for barely a minute.

"You obviously don't have a teenage sister."

Joseph's eyes narrowed. "No, but I have a mother who was so good at covering up bruises she could have been a makeup artist."

Trent rubbed his mouth. "I'm sorry about your mother. If she needs help, I'm here."

"I handled it."

"How?"

"I got bigger than he was. And stronger. Turns out he didn't like being on the wrong end of a fist."

"I hope you don't think violence is the answer."

"It depends on the question and who's asking it. I'm not a fighter. But I will protect people I care about in the best way I can."

The hint—or was it a threat?—was unmistakable. "You don't have to protect Alyssa. At least not from her family."

The teen's gaze bored into Trent. "Lots of people never do something until the day they do."

Alyssa walked into the room, sparing Trent the need to reply to that cynical comment.

"Alyssa," Joseph said, rushing to her side. He took her hands in his and in one long gaze studied her from head to toe. She'd combed her hair and washed her face. She glowed with excitement. "Are you all right?"

She nodded, and then tears filled her eyes. She jerked her hands from his and backed away. "Daddy said you don't really love me. He says you're using me and that the only reason you're being nice to me is so I'll have sex with you."

"What?" Joseph swung an accusing glare at Trent before looking back at Alyssa. "Your father is wrong. I love you."

Alyssa looked at the floor. She gnawed on her bottom lip and rubbed her hands against her thighs. "But you're cool and smart and popular. Why else would you want to be with a loser like me?"

Trent's heart dropped to his feet. His daughter sounded so defeated. "Wait a minute, Alyssa. That's not what I said."

Alyssa turned her tearstained face to his. "Yes, you did. You tried to make it sound nice, but I know what you meant. I'm not special enough for a cool boy to like me for myself. Not like Mom was. She was special enough for you to fall in love with her when she was eleven. Not like me. There's only one reason a boy would want to be with me."

What had he done? He was trying to protect her. How had he managed to destroy his little girl's faith in herself in the process?

"You're not a loser. You're the best," Joseph said. "And I do love you."

Alyssa was shaking her head while tears ran down her face.

"Think. Have I tried to have sex with you? Have I

even mentioned it?" She didn't answer, so he prodded her. "Have I?"

"No."

"Yesterday was the first time I kissed you. Right?"

"Yes."

"If I was only using you, don't you think I would have tried something before yesterday?"

She shrugged. "Maybe. I guess so."

"I know. I love you, Alyssa. Maybe your father doesn't believe it, but you should. You knew it in your heart yesterday. You only doubt me because of him. He doesn't want us to be together. He says I'm too old and he doesn't want me around you. No matter what he does, don't let him convince you that you aren't special. You are." Joseph wiped tears from her face. "You are everything that's good. Everything."

"But Daddy says—"

"I don't care what your daddy says. He's wrong."

Alyssa nodded and fell into Joseph's arms. Holding her while she cried, he glared at Trent. When she calmed, Joseph led her to the sofa and sat beside her. Although Trent wanted to straighten out the mess he'd made with Alyssa, he didn't insist the young man leave when Alyssa seemed to need him so much.

Wandering into the kitchen, Trent sank into a chair and dropped his head into his hands. When Anna died, she'd left her daughters with a huge void in their lives he knew he couldn't fill. Girls needed their mothers. Good mothers built their daughters self-esteem. Since Anna wasn't around, he thought knowing their mother was special would help them feel special. Instead, he'd made Alyssa feel inadequate. He didn't know how to make it better, but he knew he was the only one who could.

Finally, Trent returned to the living room. Joseph was

sitting beside Alyssa, holding her hand in his. She'd stopped crying and was even smiling. Her smile dimmed when she saw her father.

"I need to speak with Alyssa," he said.

"I figured you would." Joseph looked down at Alyssa. "Walk me out."

She followed him to the door. A minute later she returned. Her eyes were downcast and whatever joy she'd shown while Joseph was around had disappeared. She headed for the stairs.

"Sit down a minute, princess."

She huffed out a sigh but returned to the sofa, giving him hope he hadn't entirely ruined their relationship. She still refused to meet his eyes.

He sat beside her. "I'm sorry, Alyssa."

She shrugged.

"You're very special. Every bit as special as your mother was."

"I'll never be as pretty as she was."

Trent reeled back. "Are you kidding? You look just like her."

She shook her head, so Trent went to the bookcase and pulled out an old photo album. He used to show the pictures to the girls all the time, but over the years they'd lost interest and he'd stopped. Now he opened to a picture of Anna at her eighth grade graduation party and handed the book to Alyssa.

"That's your mom when she was about your age."

"She was so pretty."

"So are you. You look just like her."

"You think so?" Her voice was filled with disbelief and hope.

He nodded. "Your eyes, your cheekbones, your smile. Everything."

Alyssa stared at the picture and finally nodded, as if she saw the resemblance.

"And you're as special as she was. Maybe more. I never meant to make you feel you weren't. I was just afraid of how attached you're getting to Joseph."

"You don't think he loves me back."

Trent winced. "I didn't want to think about it. You may be getting older, but you're still my little girl. The idea of you being in love gives me hives."

She giggled, then sobered. "I'm not stupid. I know some boys have sex with a girl and later act like they don't know her. Joseph isn't like that."

"How do you know this?"

"Because." She looked at Trent and then away, twisting her fingers. "He's never had sex. He wants to wait, because he's going away to college and doesn't want to take chances."

"That's smart."

"I'm smart, too."

He kissed her forehead. "Yes, you are."

"So why don't you trust me?"

"I do."

"So can I date Joseph?"

"Alyssa, he's so much older than you are."

"Just three years. You're way older than Carmen."

"Carmen and I aren't dating."

Alyssa gasped. "You're not?"

"No. We're just friends."

"You don't love her?" Alyssa's voice had grown louder and shriller with each word, and now she was practically yelling.

"No."

"But you had sex with her!"

What? He definitely didn't want to discuss his sex life

with his daughter. But if he wanted her to be honest with him, he needed to be honest with her. Sometimes parenthood sucked. "Do I want to know how you know that?"

"We live in Sweet Briar. Everyone knows."

He grimaced.

"So if you don't love her, why did you have sex with her?"

"We're adults."

"That's not an answer."

"It's the only one you're getting."

"Does Carmen know you don't love her?"

She did now. "Yes."

Alyssa seemed to think about that. Thankfully, she didn't say anything else. He already felt horrible about hurting Carmen.

Alyssa hopped up. When she reached the stairs, she turned back. "Thanks for talking to me. I love you, Daddy."

Alyssa's words about Carmen stuck with Trent the rest of the day. Was Carmen in love with him? And had she thought he loved her back? If so, he might have hurt her even worse than he thought. How was he supposed to live with that?

Chapter Twenty-One

Trent parked in front of the youth center and hopped out of the car. He waved at a couple volunteers he recognized from the basketball tournament. Neither woman returned his greeting. Puzzled, he kept going until he reached the reception area. Again he was greeted coolly. What was going on?

"Daddy," Robyn cried, running across the floor and leaping into his arms. For the first time in a long while, she wasn't carrying an art project.

"How was your day?"

"Okay. I played basketball and lots of games."

"No art?"

She shook her head and frowned. "Carmen wasn't here and there wasn't anyone to help us. Joseph said he'll teach art tomorrow."

"Did he say when Carmen's coming back?"

"She isn't," Alyssa said, joining them.

"Of course she is. Remember she said she would stay for the summer? This must have something to do with her upcoming gallery show." He hoped he didn't sound as desperate as he felt. Surely Carmen wouldn't leave without saying goodbye.

"Believe what you want," Alyssa said, not giving him any hope. "We're ready to go."

"Go ahead and get in the car. I need to talk to Joni."

"Okay, but she's going to tell you the same thing. Carmen's gone."

Trent knocked on Joni's open door before stepping inside.

"How can I help you, Chief?"

Trent wasn't surprised by the chill in Joni's voice. Although he considered her a friend, she and Carmen had established a much closer relationship. "You can tell me what's going on with Carmen."

"She went home."

"Did she say why?"

"Any conversation we had is private."

"Come on, Joni."

"Come on what? Do you want me to tell you how she called me in tears? Do you need to hear how you broke her heart? If you knew you couldn't love her, why didn't you just leave her alone?"

"I never intended to hurt her."

"Well, that makes it all right, then." Joni's sarcasm cut like a knife. It was worse than the disappointment he'd seen in Alyssa's eyes.

"Do you have a number for her?"

"Not one I'm willing to share." She looked at her watch. "If you don't mind, I have work to do."

Trent left, telling himself it was for the best. Carmen deserved a man who would love her, something he could never allow himself to do.

* * *

The sun was streaking across the Manhattan skyline when Carmen finally put down her brush. She rubbed her eyes with her fists. Her shoulders and back ached from endless hours of constant work. It had taken five restless days and sleepless nights, but she'd finally worked through the worst of her sadness and heartache.

The painting she'd just finished wasn't for her upcoming show. In fact, it wouldn't leave her studio. A combination of angry reds and depressing purples, it bore no resemblance to her usual work. And yet she couldn't use the yellows and greens she preferred. She didn't need a psychiatrist to tell her the painting reflected the resentment and hurt she felt.

She closed her eyes and memories of the time she and Trent had spent together bombarded her. Although she tried to rein them in, they crashed through her defenses. Trent smiling at her as they shared her picnic lunch. His laughter as they ran through the park, trying to get the kite into the air. That had been a perfect day and a pivotal moment in their relationship. She'd felt comfortable enough to share her past without glossing over the uglier parts.

Other memories followed quickly. Walking together along the moonlit beach. Sitting on his porch swing under the stars. The basketball tournament. Making love.

A moan escaped her lips as she recalled the night she'd spent in his arms. She could still smell his masculine scent. Still taste his slightly salty skin. Still feel his muscles under her fingers. He'd been so tender and gentle with her, touching not just her flesh, but her heart. A tear slid down her cheek and she brushed it away.

A part of her had always suspected Trent didn't love her. Couldn't love her. He'd had the perfect wife. No doubt she'd become even more flawless in his mind through the years. Yet hearing him say the words had gutted Carmen. But she wasn't angry at him. She'd gone into everything with her eyes open, so if she was hurt she had only herself to blame.

Despite how it had ended, she didn't regret their time together. She'd been happy. But it was over. It was time to move on with her life. Feeling a peace that had eluded her since Trent had told her he couldn't love her, she stretched. For the first time since she'd left Sweet Briar, she knew she would be able to sleep.

Trent prowled the house, unable to sleep. For the fifth time in as many nights, he found himself sitting in his backyard staring at the predawn sky, watching as one by one the stars went out. He couldn't help but think that was a metaphor for his life.

The sun slowly crept over the horizon before bursting into glorious light. As bright as the day promised to be, the sun didn't hold a candle to the light that regularly shone in Carmen's eyes. Until he'd thoughtlessly snuffed it out. Once again guilt rocketed through him as he recalled her tears. Tears that he'd caused. Thanks to Joni, he knew those weren't the last ones she'd cried.

He shifted uneasily in the lawn chair, as if he might shake off the regrets. Unfortunately, they clung like steel vines and weren't about to let him get comfortable.

He wondered how she was. If she could sleep any better than he could. He should have left her alone. That he hadn't planned on hurting her didn't exonerate him or change the fact that he had hurt her.

Being with her had felt so right. It was as if everything in his life had settled into its proper place, giving him peace. And he'd hurt her so badly she'd left town.

He needed to make things right. More important, he had to make sure she was all right. He was going to New York.

The flight was short and the weather perfect. After checking into his hotel, he called home to make sure his girls were fine, then went in search of food. He enjoyed the best corned beef on rye of his life, then returned to his hotel to change. Art wasn't really his thing and he'd never stepped foot inside a gallery before, but this was for Carmen. Although she hadn't asked, he wanted to be there to support her. Hopefully, she would see that not only was he sorry for hurting her, but that he valued her and wanted to reestablish their relationship. He might not be in love with her, but he needed her in his life. It wouldn't be the same without her.

The gallery was a short taxi ride from his hotel. He straightened his tie and navy suit jacket before entering. The room had three-story-high ceilings, large windows and an airy feeling despite the scent of too many heavy perfumes lingering in the air. The white walls enhanced the brilliant colors of two dozen paintings. Several groups of people were walking about, conversing quietly as they studied the work. If the amount of diamonds the women wore were any indication, Carmen's work appealed to the wealthy buyer.

A black-clad waiter glided through the crowd, stopping before Trent and offering him a flute of champagne, which he declined. Stepping farther into the room, he was greeted by a smiling woman who handed him a glossy brochure containing images of Carmen's work. He preferred to look at the actual paintings, so he tucked the booklet into his jacket pocket.

He walked past people admiring various pieces of her art until he reached the back of the long, rectangular room.

Moving around a waitress carrying a tray of canapés, he stepped closer to one of the last paintings and stared. The perfectly detailed image of three little girls dancing on a lakeshore was the most amazing thing he'd ever seen. The joy on their faces evoked emotions he couldn't quite name. It was as if Carmen had painted a memory or perhaps a dream.

With his heart in his throat, he moved to the next painting, wondering if it would elicit more emotions. It did. Although this time he felt her heartbreak. It was as if she'd opened her heart and poured out her emotions on the canvas.

Longing to see Carmen consumed him and he scanned the room. And there she was. Dressed in a bright red sheath, she was a vision in a room filled with basic black dresses. She wore her hair in the waves he preferred, bouncing freely around her angelic face. She turned and smiled at a well-dressed man standing beside her. A twinge of jealousy reared its ugly head, but Trent quickly squelched it. Carmen wasn't his woman. She could speak with anyone she chose.

Of their own volition, his feet walked in Carmen's direction until he was standing directly in front of her. From a distance she looked radiant, but up close she was breathtaking. Her eyes were alight with pleasure and her cheeks flushed with joy. When she looked at him, her smile faded. He felt its loss down to his soul.

"Trent."

He wished he could greet her with a kiss. "Hello."

"What are you doing here?"

"I wanted to see you." He looked around. "Is there somewhere we can talk privately?"

"No. There's nothing left to say."

"Please, Carmen."

A gallery employee interrupted. Someone was purchasing a painting and wanted to speak with Carmen. She nodded, the look of relief on her face cutting Trent to the quick.

"So you're the chief," said the man who'd been the recipient of Carmen's smile.

Trent raised an eyebrow. In his early forties, the man was about Trent's height and build. His tailor-made suit probably cost more than Trent made in a month. Trent turned to walk away, but a hand on his shoulder stopped him. He jerked away and looked at the other man.

"I'm Damon," he said, offering his hand.

"You're Damon?" He didn't look at all like what Trent had expected. Carmen had described him as a father figure. He'd expected someone in his fifties or sixties, balding and with a potbelly, not someone fit and only a few years older than Trent was. He shook the man's hand automatically.

"You're upsetting Carmen," Damon said, his tone blunt. "You need to stay out of it."

"Not going to happen. Carmen is important to me and this reception is important to her."

"And what makes you think it's any different with me?"

Damon laughed and Trent felt his fingers curl into a fist. "Because I love her. Since you don't, I don't see why any of it matters to you."

Trent shook his head, trying to make sense of the other man's words. "She told me she thinks of you as a father."

"Feelings change."

"Is that so?" Trent couldn't even think this man was in love with Carmen. And she with him.

"Yep. We no longer think of each other as father and daughter."

Trent stiffened his spine and willed himself not to overreact as Damon continued. "Now our relationship is more like little sister and older brother."

"What?" Trent's relief so was great he could barely choke out the word.

Damon laughed. "You heard me. My question for you again is why do you care?"

Trent shrugged. Carmen might feel comfortable sharing her feelings with this man, but Trent never would. "I appreciate your concern, but I need to talk to Carmen."

"Not now."

"That's not your decision."

"You're a cop, right? You wouldn't want Carmen coming to a crime scene demanding to talk to you. This is her job. Show her the same respect. Your presence is upsetting enough. Don't make it worse."

The man was right. Trent nodded. "I'll find another time and place to talk to her."

"We were planning to go to dinner after the reception. I'll cancel and the two of you can talk."

Trent was here. She didn't know why he'd come or even how he'd found out the location of the reception. Yet there he was, masculinity personified. She forced her attention away from him and to the person who'd just spent fifteen thousand dollars on one of her paintings. Smiling, she thanked the buyer again for the purchase. Stephan, the gallery owner, gave her a discreet thumbs-up. So far, nine of her paintings had sold, and there was fierce interest in five more. Despite how well-received her work had been, she was always a bundle of nerves at shows and pleasantly surprised when people actually bought her paintings.

Ordinarily, the success of a show calmed her nerves. Not tonight. Trent was to blame. His presence set her on high alert. The sound of his voice set alarm bells ringing. Why wasn't she over him? Why was he even here? He didn't want her. He wanted Anna.

Forcing herself to focus on business, she answered questions about her work and mingled with the guests. Finally, the reception ended and the last of the stragglers headed for the exit. She'd managed to avoid Trent the entire time and was unaware of when he'd left.

Fifteen of her paintings sold. Three more were being held by interior decorators who wanted to bring in clients to see them. Stephan was ecstatic and hugged her with the enthusiasm he usually reserved for his wife.

She bade him goodbye and quickly went outside to where Damon was waiting.

Trent stood beside him.

Damon brushed his lips across her cheek. "I'm going to take a rain check on dinner so the two of you can talk."

"I don't want to talk to him."

"Then listen while he talks to you. He might say something you want to hear."

"I doubt it," she grumbled.

With a knowing wink, Damon walked away.

When Trent and Carmen were alone, she folded her arms. "So talk."

He stepped close enough to steal the breath from her lungs. "Do you mind if we go somewhere more private? Is there a restaurant near here?"

There were several restaurants nearby, but she didn't want to go to any of them. The last time she and Trent talked, she'd ended up in tears. If she broke down again, she didn't want to do it with an audience. "I don't live far from here. I guess we can talk there."

They flagged down a cab and fifteen minutes later were walking into her apartment.

"It's nice," Trent said, looking around the small living room.

She nodded her thanks. Decorated with pieces she'd collected over the years, the room was eclectic and warm.

"Is that your artwork?" he asked, crossing the room to stand in front of a painting hanging over her sofa. A little girl was standing in a field, a secret smile on her face.

"It's one of the first I ever did. I've had offers for it, but I can't make myself part with it."

"I can see why."

They were silent for a moment. She sat and indicated he should do the same. "So what did you want to talk to me about?"

"Us."

She steeled her heart. "There is no us."

"But there can be." He leaned forward, his elbows on his knees. "I miss you, Carmen. I want you in my life."

Despite her best intentions, she began to hope. "As what?"

He pushed to his feet and began pacing the room. "Why do we have to put a label on it? Why can't we just go on as we were and see where things go? That was working before."

It hadn't worked for her. At least not once he'd made his lack of feelings known.

He was standing beside her fireplace, looking as ill at ease as she felt. Bringing him here had been a mistake. She would never be able to get the image of him in her home out of her mind.

"Well?" he prompted.

Her eyes began to burn with unshed tears. She rose from the chair. "Sorry, no."

He closed the distance between them and took her hands in his. The warmth of his fingers felt so good. "I'm willing to try for more."

She snatched her hands away. "I don't want a man who is willing to try for more. I deserve better." She paused, wondering how much to disclose. Forget it. She'd tell him everything. She wasn't ashamed of how she felt. "If you haven't guessed, I'm in love with you. I didn't plan it and I don't know how it happened. I don't blame you for not feeling the same. I knew you couldn't. But I'm not set-tling for a man who still wears his wedding ring offering to try to love me."

She stared into his beautiful eyes for what would be the last time. "All my life I've been told I'm not good enough. That I was second best. I won't be second best again. And I won't settle for less than I deserve, which is a man as madly in love with me as I am with him."

"So that's it? Because I can't promise a fairy-tale end-ing we can't have anything?"

"I want it all. I want what you gave Anna." Her voice broke, but she forced herself to continue, even though she could only whisper. "I want your heart."

He shook his head. "I can't give that to you. I've been honest about that. But that doesn't mean we can't have something good."

"That's not enough."

"That's all I can do."

"No. It's all you're willing to do." Her heart was shatter-ing in a thousand pieces and she couldn't take any more. She crossed the room and opened the door. "Please leave."

"Carmen."

"Please." The tears she'd held in check began to fall. He crossed the room and stopped in front of her. He lifted a hand as if to wipe away her tears, then dropped it.

"I'm sorry, Carmen."

She closed the door behind him, wishing she could close her heart as easily.

Chapter Twenty-Two

Trent looked at the manpower report before him and threw down his pen. He didn't have the will to do paperwork now. Shoving back his chair, he stood and grabbed his keys.

Lex stood in the doorway. "Going somewhere?"

"Patrol."

Lex stepped inside and sat down. "It'll keep."

Trent huffed out a breath and dropped into his chair. "I hope this won't take long."

"That's up to you. I've gotten a lot of complaints about you from your officers, and one of your dispatchers has threatened to quit."

"Who?"

"That's not important. Ever since you got back from New York you've been in a funk. I don't know what happened between you and Carmen, but you need to get over it."

"This has nothing to do with her."

"Lie to yourself, but not to me. What, did she tell you she doesn't love you?"

Trent dropped his head into his hands. "Worse. She told me she does."

"Then what's the problem? She loves you and you love her."

"I don't love her."

"Since when?"

"Always."

"Then why are you acting like a bear with a thorn in your paw?"

"Just because I don't love her doesn't mean I don't miss her." In a short time, she'd become important to him. Her absence created a giant hole in his life. In his heart.

"Like you miss Anna?"

"Yes. No. I don't know."

"Then maybe you should figure it out before half your department walks out." Lex stood. "Anna's gone. Carmen is here. And she cares for you. If you play your cards right, you can get her back before she realizes she could do better with me."

Trent shook his head, unable to laugh at Lex's joke. The idea of Carmen with anyone else turned his stomach. The very thought of another man having the right to touch her curdled his blood. But if he wasn't going to share her life, she would eventually find someone else to love. He'd be left living half a life, remembering the happiness he'd had, but knowing he'd thrown away the promise of more.

He left his office and crossed the reception area to where his dispatcher sat. She glanced at him, then instead of smiling and entertaining him with stories of her grandkids as she usually did, she rolled her eyes and busied herself with paperwork. He really had been a jerk this past week. "I'm sorry. I've had some things on my mind, but I shouldn't have taken my bad mood out on you."

She was silent for a long moment and then smiled.

"Don't worry about it, Chief. We all have our bad days. Shall I pass the word that our boss and friend is back?"

"Yeah, although I still owe everyone a personal apology. Order lunch from the diner for yourself and everyone on duty and charge it to me. I'm going to be gone for about an hour. There's something I need to handle."

In miles, the drive to the cemetery was short. But in his heart, it was one of the longest he'd ever made. His stomach churned as he thought of the goodbye he had to say. When he reached Anna's grave, Trent allowed himself to remember the times they had shared over the years. From falling in love, to dating, to the birth of their children. Their life together had been wonderful and he had been happy. But that time was over. Although he would never forget, it was time to look ahead.

He knelt, tears burning the back of his eyes. "I loved you, Anna. You were the best part of my life. I'll never forget you." He wiped his damp cheeks. "I've met someone. You'd like Carmen. She's kind and sweet and loves the girls. Amazingly enough, she loves me, too. I messed up with her before, but I'm going to get it right this time."

He raised his left hand. Slowly, he removed the ring Anna had placed there and slipped it into his shirt pocket. The past was over. Now he had to get started on his future.

He was going back to New York.

Trent paced the sidewalk in front of Carmen's apartment in the fading sunlight. He'd paid an exorbitant amount of money for a cramped last-row seat on the first plane to New York. He hadn't bothered reserving a hotel room but had rushed over here as soon as he'd landed. If things worked out, he would be staying with Carmen. If not... He wouldn't think about that. Failure wasn't an option.

His girls had been surprised when he'd told them he was

returning to New York. Once he'd explained his plan, they jumped on board. Robyn had cheered and raced around the house, clapping her hands. It had taken forever to calm her down. Alyssa had warned him not to blow it this time.

He had no interest in wrecking things again. He couldn't believe he'd offered Carmen so little of his heart. She'd been right to turn him down. She did deserve better. He'd get it right this time. Of course, he couldn't do anything until she came home.

After another twenty minutes of sitting on her stoop, he began to wonder if he'd made a tactical error. He'd assumed she was in the city and would be home. It hadn't occurred to him that he would have to track her down. He was contemplating his next move when he saw her walking down the street.

She was so beautiful. Dressed as she was in a long white dress that flowed around her ankles, he envisioned her as his bride, walking down the aisle to him. All that she needed was a bouquet of flowers like the one he'd bought from a kiosk. He might be getting ahead of himself, but since he knew what he wanted he didn't want to waste time.

He stood and walked toward her, too impatient to wait for her to reach him. That was when she looked up and saw him. She stopped walking and blinked. Lifting her chin and throwing back her shoulders, she waited. A knot of dread formed in his stomach. She wasn't going to make this easy. But then, he didn't deserve easy.

"What are you doing here?"

He offered her the flowers. When she didn't move to take them, he let his arm fall to his side. He decided to skip his speech and cut to the chase. "I came to see you."

"Why? I thought we'd settled things last time you were here."

"Did you?"

Shaking her head, she moved around him. Apparently, that was the wrong answer. She reached her brownstone and started up the stairs. If she stepped inside, he would lose her forever. He'd die if that happened. Not physically, but his heart would never be the same.

He hurried after her and grabbed her arm. Turning her gently, he gazed into her eyes. "I came back because I love you."

"You love Anna."

This was his last chance to get this right. There wouldn't be a third. "Yes. A part of me always will. She was my first love and the mother of my children. But she is my past. I'm hoping you'll be my present and future."

Carmen shook her head. "Don't do this to me. Please. I know you mean well, but my heart can't take it."

"Can't take what?"

"The hurt that will come when you realize you don't feel the way you think."

"You're wrong. I love you just as much as I ever loved Anna." He looked into Carmen's eyes and bared his soul. "I tried to deny my feelings because I was afraid."

"Of what?"

"Of losing you. I knew how much it would hurt if I ever lost you, so I pushed you away and told myself I didn't love you. Couldn't be in love with you. But living without you hurts as much as losing you in the future would."

Her voice was a trembling whisper. "Don't say it if you don't mean it. That would be cruel."

He cupped her face and caressed her soft skin. "I know you don't have reason to trust me, but I'm being honest. I love you with everything inside me."

"Promise?"

That whispered word was a fist to his gut. He'd been so busy protecting his heart that he'd broken hers. "I swear."

She leaned into his hand. "Okay."

He closed his eyes and breathed a sigh of relief.

"So where do we go from here?" she asked.

He extended the flowers to her again. This time she smiled and accepted them. "You're willing to take the bouquet?"

She nodded.

"How about this?" He pulled an emerald-cut diamond ring from his pocket and got down on one knee. He'd scoured countless Charlotte jewelry stores until he'd found a ring as perfect as Carmen.

"What are you doing?"

"I'm asking you to marry me. I'm asking you to be Alyssa and Robyn's stepmother. I know things are still tense with your family and might never change, but my girls and I would love it if you became a part of the Knight family. Come back to Sweet Briar with me to live. Forever."

"Yes, oh yes."

He slid the ring onto her finger and rose, pulling her into his arms and kissing her with all the love in his heart, grateful for another chance. Carmen had taken his once bleak future and painted it with bright colors of love.

* * * * *

More SWEET BRIAR SWEETHEARTS
stories coming soon from Kathy Douglass
and Mills & Boon Cherish!

MILLS & BOON®

Cherish™

EXPERIENCE THE ULTIMATE RUSH OF FALLING IN LOVE

A sneak peek at next month's titles...

In stores from 9th February 2017:

- **Proposal for the Wedding Planner** – Sophie Pembroke *and* **Fortune's Second-Chance Cowboy** – Marie Ferrarella
- **Return of Her Italian Duke** – Rebecca Winters *and* **The Marine Makes His Match** – Victoria Pade

In stores from 23rd February 2017:

- **The Millionaire's Royal Rescue** – Jennifer Faye *and* **Just a Little Bit Married** – Teresa Southwick
- **A Bride for the Brooding Boss** – Bella Bucannon *and* **Kiss Me, Sheriff!** – Wendy Warren

---

Just can't wait?
Buy our books online before they hit the shops!
www.millsandboon.co.uk

Also available as eBooks.

MILLS & BOON®

EXCLUSIVE EXTRACT

Pastry chef Gemma Rizzo never expected
to see Vincenzo Gagliardi again. And now
he's not just the duke who left her
broken-hearted... he's her boss!

Read on for a sneak preview of
RETURN OF HER ITALIAN DUKE

Since he'd returned to Italy, thoughts of Gemma had
come back full force. At times he'd been so preoccupied,
the guys were probably ready to give up on him. To
think that after all this time and searching for her, she
was right here. Bracing himself, he took the few steps
necessary to reach Takis's office.

With the door ajar he could see a polished-looking
woman in a blue-and-white suit with dark honey-blond
hair falling to her shoulders. She stood near the desk
with her head bowed, so he couldn't yet see her profile.

Vincenzo swallowed hard to realize Gemma was no
longer the teenager with short hair he used to spot when
she came bounding up the stone steps of the *castello*
from school wearing her uniform. She'd grown into a
curvaceous woman.

"Gemma." He said her name, but it came out gravelly.

A sharp intake of breath reverberated in the office.
She wheeled around. Those unforgettable brilliant green
eyes with the darker green rims fastened on him. A

stillness seemed to surround her. She grabbed hold of the desk.

"Vincenzo—I—I think I must be hallucinating."

"I'm in the same condition." His gaze fell on the lips he'd kissed that unforgettable night. Their shape hadn't changed, nor the lovely mold of her facial features.

She appeared to have trouble catching her breath. "What's going on? I don't understand."

"Please sit down and I'll tell you."

He could see she was trembling. When she didn't do his bidding, he said, "I have a better idea. Let's go for a ride in my car. It's parked out front. We'll drive to the lake at the back of the estate, where no one will bother us. Maybe by the time we reach it, your shock will have worn off enough to talk to me."

Hectic color spilled into her cheeks. "Surely you're joking. After ten years of silence, you suddenly show up here this morning, honestly thinking I would go anywhere with you?"

Don't miss
RETURN OF HER ITALIAN DUKE
by Rebecca Winters

Available March 2017
www.millsandboon.co.uk

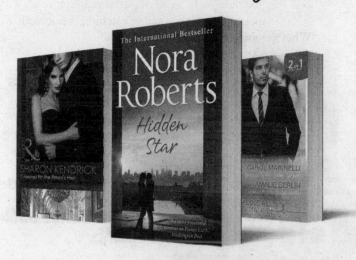